Was he really prepared to track down every female guest until he found a green-eyed redhead with a sexy little mole on her right hip?

Of course not, because even if he had the time or the energy for such an endeavor, the discovery of her true identity would change nothing. Because he'd known when he invited her back to his room that they could never be anything more than strangers in the night.

So why was he wishing for something different now? Why was he fantasizing about an impossible reunion with a woman he didn't even know?

His future was already laid out for him and last night had been only a temporary and forbidden deviation from the path that had been set for him at birth. It was time to set himself back on that path and be the king his country needed.

It was time to meet his bride.

Dear Reader,

Royal Holiday Bride is my sixth title in the Reigning Men series, but the first that starts with a bona fide princess.

I remember reading fairy tales as a child and being captivated by the idea of finding my own prince someday. As I grew up, I was less enchanted by the prospect of meeting a real blueblood and more interested in meeting a man who embodied princely characteristics. (And not only did I meet one, but I married him!)

But for a woman who is already a princess, what does she dream about? Surprisingly, Princess Marissa Leandres of Tesoro del Mar doesn't have great expectations—until she meets the newly crowned King of Ardena. Then the sparks start to fly and the princess begins to hope that the chemistry between them might lead to a fabulous holiday wedding…and a happily-ever-after.

I hope you enjoy their story.

Best,

Brenda Harlen

ROYAL HOLIDAY BRIDE

BRENDA HARLEN

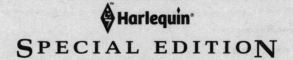

Harlequin®

SPECIAL EDITION

ISBN-13: 978-0-373-65642-4

ROYAL HOLIDAY BRIDE

Other titles by Brenda Harlen available in ebook

BRENDA HARLEN

grew up in a small town, surrounded by books and imaginary friends. Although she always dreamed of being a writer, she chose to follow a more traditional career path first. After two years of practicing as an attorney (including an appearance in front of the Supreme Court of Canada), she gave up her "real" job to be a mom and to try her hand at writing books. Three years, five manuscripts and another baby later, she sold her first book—an RWA Golden Heart winner—to Silhouette Books.

Brenda lives in southern Ontario with her real-life husband/hero, two heroes-in-training and two neurotic dogs. She is still surrounded by books (too many books, according to her children) and imaginary friends, but she also enjoys communicating with real people. Readers can contact Brenda by email at brendaharlen@yahoo.com or by snail mail c/o Harlequin Books, 233 Broadway, Suite 1001, New York, NY 10279.

To Sharon & Ken May~

When I created the fictional island of Tesoro del Mar for the Reigning Men series, I was looking for a make-believe paradise. When you invited me to Exuma, I discovered that paradise is real—and it's in the Bahamas.

Thank you both so much for sharing it with me!

Chapter One

Princess Marissa Leandres of Tesoro del Mar had a plan.

If her plan seemed a little desperate, well, that was probably because she *was* desperate. For too many years, she'd been a good princess, behaving as was expected of her, careful not to make waves in the family or do anything that might result in a scandal. After all, her brother, Cameron, had created more than enough of those.

But time was running out and if she had any hope of taking control of her life and her future, she had to make a move. And she knew she would never have a better opportunity than tonight's masquerade ball.

What better way for a princess to shed the restrictions inherent to her title and all of her own personal inhibitions than to be someone else—at least for one night?

Still, she couldn't deny that she was nervous. Actually, she was more than nervous—she was terrified. But she was also determined.

She hadn't planned to be a twenty-eight-year-old virgin. As a teenager experiencing the first stirrings of physical attraction, she'd been cautious. Not that she'd thought of her virginity as any great prize, but she hadn't been anxious to throw it away, either—especially not with the possibility of a reporter or photographer lurking around every corner.

While a lot of her friends boasted about going "all the way," she'd been content to wait, at least until she met someone really special. Unfortunately, that special someone never did cross her path, and now her mother was ready to offer her as a virgin sacrifice to Anthony Volpini, the Duke of Bellemoro.

Marissa shuddered at the thought. No way was she going to let that happen. She'd shared one brief kiss with Anthony a few years back, and the memory of that lip-lock was not a pleasant one. The prospect of experiencing anything more intimate with the lecherous duke made her skin crawl. So tonight, she was dressed as Juno. And the goddess knew what she wanted.

As she made her way toward the ballroom, the elegantly engraved invitation trembled in her fingers. Her first test would be at the door, where her cousin and his wife, Prince Rowan and Princess Lara, would be greeting each and every guest. If she could get past them—

No, she wouldn't let herself think *if*. She had to be confident. She had to ignore the butterflies frantically winging around inside her tummy and refuse to think about all the reasons she should abort her plan—and she knew there were many. She couldn't have second thoughts about what she was doing, because if she didn't go through with it tonight, she would forever be a helpless pawn in her mother's unending games.

Drawing in a slow, deep breath, she took a step forward as the line of guests advanced. She couldn't help but smile when she caught a glimpse of herself in one of the antique mirrors that lined the halls. She'd worried that her plan would fail, that she would somehow be recognized, but as she curtsied to the prince regent and his wife and neither of them showed so much as a flicker of recognition, her butterflies began to settle.

Really, she had nothing to worry about. With the auburn wig, emerald-colored contacts and elaborate mask covering half of her face, her own mother wouldn't be able to identify her. Not to mention that the gold sandals on her feet added a full four inches to her usually petite five-foot-four-inch frame.

The one-shoulder toga-style gown hugged her breasts, nipped in at her waist and flowed to the floor with a slit halfway up her thigh on one side. It was more suggestive than revealing, but it made her feel sexy and daring—and nothing at all like the demure and conservative Princess Marissa.

She liked sensual fabrics and bright colors, but she didn't often wear them in public. She preferred to blend into the background, unnoticed by the paparazzi that had always shadowed her brother's every move. She'd certainly never worn anything so vibrant and bold, and she knew there was no way she could hide in the background in this outfit. But tonight she didn't want to hide—she wanted to be noticed. She wanted to be wanted.

Tonight, "the prim princess" was finally going to lose her virginity.

Dante Romero hated costume balls. He felt ridiculous enough in the finery he was required to wear for state functions without having to dress up and pretend to be someone else. As if being born a prince hadn't required him to do enough role-playing on a daily basis, he was now trapped in the role of King of Ardena.

It was his birthright and his burden, and one he hadn't expected to assume so early. Unfortunately, his father's health had rapidly deteriorated over the past few years to the point that King Benedicto and his advisers—and especially his doctors—had agreed it would be best for the country if he passed the throne to his son. It was a position Dante had been groomed for throughout his entire life, his inescapable destiny.

Not that he was looking to escape. He acknowledged and understood his responsibilities to his family, his people and his country. But he was barely thirty-two years old and he'd always thought he'd have more time before he had to accept those responsibilities—more time to be free before he gave his people a queen.

But his father had been unrelenting. He hadn't worried too much about his reputation as a playboy prince, but he was the king now and his country needed a queen. He needed a partner to share his life and a mother for his children—the future heirs to the throne.

That was one of the primary reasons he was in Tesoro del Mar now—not just to shake a few hands and smile for some photo ops, but to meet Princess Marissa Leandres, the only daughter of the Princess Royal and a cousin of the prince regent. His father was optimistic that he would find the princess "acceptable enough" to consider issuing a proposal of marriage, which would go a long way toward strengthening the ties between their respective countries.

It was, Dante understood, as good a reason as any for a king to choose a bride. Unlike the childhood song that claimed "first comes love, then comes marriage," Dante knew that it was more likely "first comes coronation, then comes marriage." The official ceremony had taken place only a few weeks earlier, and now the clock was ticking.

And so, at his father's insistence, he'd paid a thousand dollars for a ticket to this masquerade ball to benefit the

Port Augustine Children's Hospital and dressed himself up like Jupiter, just because Benedicto was certain that Princess Marissa would be in attendance and because he had yet to figure out how to refuse anything his ailing father asked of him.

"She's not unattractive," his mother had informed him, although she'd seemed slightly less enthusiastic than her husband about the idea of the Tesorian princess as her son's bride. "Just a little more conservative than the women you usually date, but she is always stylish and well put together."

Unwilling to rely on his mother's description, he'd done some research on his own. Finding pictures of the princess hadn't been very difficult—though she wasn't frequently on the covers of the tabloids, she did make public appearances for noteworthy causes. It seemed that the Port Augustine Children's Hospital was one of her favorites.

He would agree that she wasn't unattractive. In fact, when he studied her face more closely, he realized that she was actually quite beautiful, if not the type of woman who would ordinarily catch his eye. Medium height, average build, dark hair usually tied back in a braid or secured in a knot at the base of her neck. Her eyes were also dark, her smile as unobtrusive as the rest of her.

It shouldn't have been too difficult to pick her out of a crowd, except when the crowd was attired in fancy costumes and elaborate masks. As Dante looked around the ballroom of the royal palace, he realized that he was surrounded by gods and goddesses and various mythological creatures, some that he recognized but many more than he did not. Even the staff were in costume: the waiters as slaves and the security guards as gladiators.

It was as if he'd stepped into another world, and he had to give credit to the decorators for their efforts. The boundary of the dance floor was marked by tall Roman-style columns wrapped in green ivy and twinkling lights. Beyond the dance floor were round tables covered in white linen with laurel wreath centerpieces. Marble pedestals topped with busts of ancient philosophers had been placed around the perimeter of the room.

Some of the guests were in formal attire and carried simple stick masks as a nod to the theme; others had elaborate costumes and face decorations that ensured they remained anonymous. For Dante, the one benefit of being unrecognizable in his costume was that he'd been able to forgo having bodyguards flanking him as he moved through the crowd.

He stepped out of Medusa's path and fought against a smile as she turned to give a blatant once-over to a centaur. He decided that even if he didn't manage to locate Princess Marissa, it wouldn't be a boring night. But he wasn't willing to give up on his mission just yet. He scanned the crowd again, looking for someone who was trying to blend into the background—an observer rather than a participant. The harder he looked, the more convinced he became that his task was futile.

And then he saw her.

The dress was of the richest emerald where it was gathered at one shoulder, with the color gradually transitioning from green to blue until it became a vivid sapphire at her ankles. Her hair spilled down her back, a luxurious cascade of silky red curls. Enormous hammered-gold earrings dangled from her ears and wide bracelets of the same style glinted at both wrists.

Her mask was an elaborate design studded with blue-and-green jewels with a fan of peacock feathers on one side; behind it, her brilliant green eyes sparkled. Her glossy lips were lush and full and curved in a tempting smile. Her skin was pale and dusted with gold. The slope of her shoulders was graceful and sexy.

Lust shot through his veins, as strong and fierce as any bolt of lightning his namesake might have thrown down from the heavens. He forgot about his mission to find the Tesorian princess and made his way across the room to her.

He bowed; she curtsied.

"Juno," he acknowledged with a nod.

Those luscious lips curved. "Jupiter?"

"Isn't it obvious?"

She gave him a slow once-over, her emerald eyes skimming over the gold-trimmed purple toga, gold breastplate, down to the sandals on his feet. "The ruler of the gods is customarily depicted with a beard."

"I'm a man for whom practicality trumps convention," he told her.

"The facial hair was itchy," she guessed.

"And you are a woman who is obviously as smart as she is beautiful."

"I know that Jupiter had a lightning bolt. I didn't know that he had such a glib tongue."

"There's probably a lot about me that you don't know," he told her. "But if you would do me the honor of sharing a dance, we could start to fill in some of the blanks."

"I'd like that," she said.

She placed her hand in his, and he felt the jolt again.

Her gaze flew to his, and he saw the same awareness—the same desire—in her eyes that was coursing through his blood.

He lifted her hand, touched his lips to the back of it.

Her breath caught in her throat and her eyes widened.

He drew her closer, dropped his voice. "Or we could skip the dance."

She shook her head. "A tempting offer, but I want to dance…at least for now."

"And later?" he queried, leading her onto the dance floor.

Her lips curved in a slow, sexy smile that made his heart pound. "We'll figure that out as we go."

He was a good dancer, Marissa noted. He moved easily, naturally, and it felt so good to be held in his arms, close to his body. Her heart was pounding and her blood was humming. For the first time since she'd set her plan in motion, she started to believe that she could go through with it.

If she could be with Jupiter.

That this man had chosen to come to the ball dressed as her mythological mate was nothing more than a coincidence, she knew that. And yet, in her heart, she believed it was a sign that she was doing the right thing.

Or maybe it was just her hormones, because she honestly couldn't ever remember responding to a man as immediately and intensely as she'd responded to this one.

She tipped her head back, smiled when she met his gaze. She'd danced with a lot of men whose eyes had roamed the dance floor, looking for their next partner, their next conquest. But Jupiter seemed interested only in her, and for a woman who was used to standing on the sidelines, being the center of such focused attention was absolutely exhilarating.

Though his face was half-covered by a gold-colored mask, there was no disguising the strength or masculinity of his features. His eyes were as dark as espresso and surrounded by thick lashes, his jaw was strong and square, his lips exquisitely shaped and quick to curve.

"So why Jupiter?" she asked him now.

"Why would I choose the identity of any one god when I could be the ruler of the gods?" he countered.

"Lofty ambitions," she mused.

For just a second, she thought she saw a shadow cross his eyes. But then he smiled, and everything inside of her quivered.

"I would expect the consort of the king to have similarly grand desires," he noted.

She didn't think his use of the word *desires* was either inadvertent or inappropriate. She had very specific plans for this night, and while she didn't think they were particularly grand, she was determined to see them through.

"You don't honestly expect me to confess my grandest desires to a stranger on the dance floor, do you?" she challenged.

"But I'm not a stranger," he pointed out, leading her away from the crowd as the song ended. "I'm your mythological mate."

He plucked two glasses of champagne from the tray of a waiter and passed one to her.

She murmured her thanks and lifted the glass to her lips to soothe her suddenly parched throat. It was easy to flirt with him on the dance floor when they were surrounded by other dancers. But now, even though there were probably five hundred people in the ballroom, she felt as if they were alone. And the nerves tying knots in her stomach were equal parts anticipation and apprehension.

She had barely finished half of her champagne when she was approached by a Minotaur. Ballroom protocol dictated that an invitation not be refused, so she let him lead her back to the dance floor. After the Minotaur, she danced with Apollo, then with a senator. Each time she made her way around the dance floor past the table where she'd left Jupiter, she saw him watching her.

She felt like the belle of the ball and she had a wonderful time dancing and chatting with all of them, more comfortable in her anonymity than she'd ever been as Princess Marissa. But all the while, she was anxious to return to Jupiter.

"I was beginning to feel neglected," he said when she

finally escaped the dance floor and made her way back to him again.

"My apologies," she said sincerely, accepting the fresh glass of champagne he offered.

"No need to apologize," he assured her, leading her away from the crowd and onto the balcony. "It's understandable that every man in attendance would want a turn on the dance floor with the most beautiful woman here."

"There's that glib tongue again," she noted.

He maneuvered her into the shadows. "Do you believe in destiny?"

"I believe we make our own destiny," she said, and reminded herself that this was the destiny she had chosen. To take control of her life and her future.

"And I believe our paths were meant to cross tonight."

She wanted to think that he sounded sincere, but even if it was nothing more than a well-worn line, even if he was just looking for a quick hookup, wasn't that what she wanted, too? Wasn't that what she *needed* to prove that she was capable of controlling her own destiny?

"And now that our paths have crossed," she said, "where do we go from here?"

Dante wasn't entirely sure how to answer her question, except that he knew he wasn't going to walk away from the lovely goddess. Not just yet.

He knew nothing about her and she knew nothing about him, and maybe the anonymity was part of the attraction. He'd been born in a castle and raised from the cradle to understand that he would rule his country one day. It was a birthright that carried with it tremendous responsibility—and relentless public scrutiny. Everything he did was fodder for the tabloids. Every decision he made was documented and analyzed. Every woman he dated was subjected to background checks and media attention.

For the first time in as long as he could remember, he wasn't a royal representative of Ardena. It was as if he'd completely shed that identity when he'd donned the costume of the Roman god. And then he'd spotted his goddess.

He didn't know if he believed in destiny, but he did believe that she'd felt that same instantaneous tug of attraction he'd experienced when their eyes met across the room. And he hoped they would have a chance to explore that attraction.

So he replied to her question with one of his own. "Where do you want to go?"

She tilted her head, studying him with steady green eyes as she considered her response. "Are you married?"

"No." His response was quick, vehement.

Her lips twitched, as if she was trying not to smile. "Engaged?"

"No," he said again. "There's no one."

She continued to hold his gaze as she finished off her champagne. When the glass was empty, he set it aside and took her hands in his, noting the absence of any rings on the third finger of her left hand. "How about you? Boyfriend? Lover?"

She shook her head and her earrings glinted in the moonlight. "Completely unattached," she assured him.

"I'm very glad to hear that," he said, and lowered his head to kiss her.

Her lips were as soft as he'd suspected, and sweetly yielding. And the flavor of her lips buzzed through his veins, more potent than the champagne he'd drunk and more addictive than anything he'd ever tasted.

She neither pulled away nor moved closer, and he sensed a certain amount of both caution and curiosity in her response. He couldn't blame her for being wary—he was a stranger and they were alone in the shadows—but he didn't want her to be afraid. So he held his escalating desire firmly in check and forced himself to move slowly.

He touched his tongue tentatively to the seam of her lips, once, twice. The second time, her lips parted for him. When he dipped inside, she brushed his tongue with her own.

He wanted to pull her into his arms, to hold her tight against his body. He wanted to feel the soft press of her breasts against his chest, to let her feel the hard proof of his desire for her. He knew what he wanted—he wanted *her*. But he sensed that she was still undecided, and he was more than happy to take whatever time was needed to convince her that she wanted him, too.

Thankfully, she seemed willing to be convinced. When he released her hands and inched closer to her, she didn't protest. When he slid his hands from her waist to her breasts, she only sighed and pressed closer to him. It was all the encouragement he needed. The fabric of her costume was almost gossamer thin, and he could clearly feel the pattern of the lace on her bra. Through the lace, he traced circles around the peaks of her nipples, felt them pucker in response to his touch.

She gasped and shuddered, but didn't pull away. He eased his lips from hers and skimmed them along her jaw, down her throat, over the curve of her collarbone. The soft, sexy noises that sounded in her throat made his blood pound and his body ache.

Maybe this was crazy. It was certainly beyond scandalous. Anyone could wander out from the ballroom as easily as they had done, but he didn't care. He experienced a heady sense of freedom that he'd never known before, trusting that even if someone did venture out onto the balcony, they wouldn't catch the king of Ardena in a compromising position. Because he wasn't the king of Ardena right now—he was Jupiter, and making love with Juno seemed like the most natural thing in the world.

He tore his mouth from hers and drew in a deep, shuddering breath to say, "Come upstairs with me."

It was a plea as much as a demand, and there was only one answer Marissa wanted to give. She would follow him to the ends of the earth if he would keep doing what he'd been doing, if he could make those exquisite sensations ricocheting through her body never stop. But even with lust clouding her mind, something in his words gave her pause.

She'd been on the verge of saying "yes." She'd been on the verge of letting him take her right there on the balcony. Because she'd thought he was an anonymous stranger. But he hadn't said *come home with me* or *come back to my hotel.* He'd said *come upstairs with me.* And if he was staying at the palace, he had to have some kind of connection to the prince regent.

She drew back, tried to catch her breath and focus her thoughts. "You have a room…here at the palace?"

He hesitated, as if only now understanding the implications of his words. But then he said, "I'm visiting with a friend who is well acquainted with the minister of foreign affairs. He arranged for our accommodations."

It was a logical explanation and not one that would concern most women. Of course, most other women weren't closely related to the minister of foreign affairs.

She exhaled slowly, reconsidering his invitation. But if the connection to her brother was only through a friend of his, then this…interlude, she decided for lack of a better term, could remain anonymous. Which meant that his revelation didn't require her to abort her plan. At least not yet.

"That seems rather convenient," she said lightly.

He brushed his lips against hers again. "Or maybe it's destiny."

She smiled and splayed her palms on his breastplate. She could feel the ridges of the storm-cloud design beneath her fingertips, but what she wanted to feel was the warmth of his bare flesh. She wanted to explore every inch of him, with her hands and her lips. It was a shockingly bold desire for a woman with zero sexual experience, and a desire that she didn't want to deny any longer.

For the first time in her life, she wanted a man without hesitation. Maybe it was foolish, maybe it was irrefutable proof that she had set upon a desperate course, but it was true. She wanted to be with *this* man. She wanted him to kiss her again, she wanted to feel his lips on hers, his hands on her body, his naked flesh against hers.

She whispered against his lips, "Lead the way."

Chapter Two

As they made their way through the maze of hallways to the third floor of the north wing, Marissa's apprehension increased.

Could she do this? Could she really make love with a stranger? She wanted to—and not just because she was determined to finally lose her virginity, but because she wanted this man as she'd never wanted anyone before. Because he'd made her feel things she'd never felt before.

But what if she got scared? What if she stepped into his room and he pressed her up against the wall and shoved his tongue down her throat and—

She jolted when he took her hand.

Behind the gold mask that covered half of his face, his gaze was hot and intense, but when he spoke, his voice was carefully neutral. "If this isn't what you want—"

"No," she interrupted quickly, shoving aside the unpleasant memory of the Duke of Bellemoro. "It is."

"Good," he said, and slipped his arms around her waist to draw her close. He lowered his head and kissed her again.

He truly was an exceptional kisser, teasing her lips, coaxing her response. As their tongues danced and mated, she felt as if she could be content to continue kissing him forever. But contentment quickly gave way to desire, and desire to need.

"Maybe we should take this inside," he suggested against her lips.

She hadn't even realized they were still in the hall. What was it about this man that he could make her lose all concept of time and place? And not even care that she'd done so?

He kept one arm around her as he slipped the old-fashioned key into the lock and pushed open the door, and he was kissing her again when he steered her inside.

She was too busy enjoying the sensation of his hands on her body to wonder how he'd scored the corner suite that was usually reserved for state visitors of the highest rank. Too preoccupied to appreciate that the thick rug on the floor of the formal sitting room was an antique Savonnerie, or that the mullioned windows were draped with heavy velvet curtains. But she did notice the massive Chippendale four-poster bed with its pale blue silk cover and mountain of pillows when he steered her into the bedroom.

"One moment," he said, and released her long enough to light the trio of candles on the rosewood bedside table.

"I wouldn't have taken you for a romantic," she admitted.

"There are times when romantic gestures are called for." He took her hand again, brought it to his lips. "I would say this is one of them."

"You've already succeeded in luring me to your room," she reminded him.

"So I have." His quick grin was sexy and satisfied as he drew her into his arms again. "And now that I have you here…how about some champagne?"

She blinked. "Champagne?"

"Sure, I could call downstairs and ask them to send up a bottle—or we could get something to eat, if you're hungry."

She shook her head. "I don't want anything but you."

"And here I was trying to show some self-restraint."

"Why?"

"Because if I didn't, we'd already be naked and in the middle of that big bed right now."

"I want to see you naked," she said and reached for the hooks that held his breastplate in place. It was heavier than she'd expected, and it nearly slipped out of her grasp before he took the armor from her and set it aside.

"Same goes." He unfastened the braided gold rope at her waist, let it fall to the floor, then turned his attention to the twisted fabric at her shoulder. As he worked the knot, his fingertips brushed her bare skin and yearning flooded through her.

When the fastening was untied, the silky gown slid down the length of her body to pool at her feet so that she stood before him in only her mask, lacy sapphire bra, matching bikini panties and the gold-colored sandals.

His gaze skimmed over her, from her shoulders to her toes and back again, slowly, hungrily. "You're even more beautiful than I anticipated."

"And you're still mostly dressed," she noted.

He unclipped his leg guards, kicked off his sandals and tugged the tunic over his head. As she watched him strip away the various pieces of his costume, she couldn't help but think that he looked even more like a god without the period enhancements.

His skin was darkly tanned—apparently all over—and stretched taut over glorious muscles. His chest was broad and smooth, and she instinctively reached out to lay her palms against the warm flesh. She felt the sizzle spread through her veins and reverberate low in her belly.

He reached for the tie at the side of her mask, but she turned her head away. Above the top of his, she saw his brows lift.

"I'm more comfortable being Juno," she explained.

His smile was tinged with amusement and desire. "Then you won't mind if I keep mine on, too?"

She suspected it was going to be a little awkward, making love while both of them were wearing masks. But she knew it was the only way she would be able to follow through with her plan. She had no objection to removing all of her clothes so long as her face remained covered, because as much as she wanted to be naked with him, she couldn't risk her identity being exposed.

"No," she responded to his question. "In fact, I'd prefer it."

"Okay," he agreed.

She exhaled slowly as her hands slid downward. Her fingertips traced over the rippling muscles of his abdomen to the top of his fitted briefs, then dipped inside. He groaned when her fingers wrapped around him, and she had a moment of worry when she registered the size and strength of him. He was huge and rock hard, and the thought of his body joining with hers made her shiver with anticipation.

"You're going to obliterate what's left of my self-restraint," he warned her.

She tipped her head back to brush her lips against his. "Good."

He cupped his hands beneath her buttocks and lifted her off the ground in a move that was so quick and unexpected, her breath whooshed out of her lungs. He tumbled her back onto the bed, the full length of his body pressing against hers, and she gasped with shock and pleasure.

Then his mouth was on hers again, hot and hungry. He

wasn't coaxing so much as demanding now, and she was more than happy to give him what he wanted, what they both needed. She ran her hands over his shoulders, down his arms, relishing the feel of his flesh beneath her fingertips. She arched beneath him, eager for more, for everything. He nibbled on her bottom lip, and she sighed again as pleasure drowned out caution and reason and everything else. She had no thoughts of anything but this man and this moment, no need for anything more. And then she had no thoughts at all as her mind gave way to the bliss of sensation.

She was everything Dante had imagined…and more. Beautiful and passionate and so incredibly responsive. And she was his—if only for this one night.

He stroked his hands slowly down her torso, a careful study of delectable feminine curves. From the sexy slope of her shoulders…to the lushness of her breasts…to the indent of her waist…the flare of her hips…then down those long, shapely legs to the laces of her sandals.

He broke the kiss and reluctantly levered himself off of her. Her eyelids flickered, opened, and she propped herself up on her elbows. He touched a fingertip to her lips, to silence any questions or protests. She said nothing, but watched him curiously.

He tugged on the lace that was tied just below her knee, then slowly unwrapped the cord. His fingers traced lightly over her skin as he unwound it, and he heard the catch of her breath. He took his time removing the first sandal, but when he dropped it to the floor, he still held on to her foot. It was narrow and slender and incredibly sexy. He stroked a finger along the arch and felt her shiver. He lifted her foot higher, kissed her ankle, then let his lips skim up her calf to her knee.

He repeated the same process with her other sandal, her other leg. Then he propped her feet on the edge of the mat-

tress so that her knees were bent and lowered his head between her thighs to kiss her through the thin barrier of lace.
She gasped, as if shocked by the intimacy of his mouth on
her. But she made no protest when he slid his hands beneath
her buttocks, tilting her hips forward to remove her panties.

He used his thumbs to part the slick folds that protected
her womanly core and flicked his tongue over her. Once.
Twice. She sucked in a breath, then let it out in a rush. He
teased her mercilessly, alternating quick strokes with slow
circles until she was whimpering. Then he teased her some
more, relentlessly driving her toward the ultimate pinnacle
of pleasure and leisurely easing back again. When he was
certain that she could take no more—when her heels were
digging into the mattress and her hands were fisted in the
covers and her breath was coming in short, shallow gasps—
he pushed her over the edge.

She was still shuddering with the aftereffects of her climax
as he made his way up her body. He unfastened the clasp
at the front of her bra and pushed the lacy cups aside. He
paused, taking a moment to enjoy the glorious nakedness of
her long, lean body stretched out on his bed.

Her breasts were perfectly shaped and centered with rosy-
pink nipples that he ached to touch, taste, savor. He dipped
his head and swirled his tongue around one turgid peak,
while his thumb traced the same path around the other. She
cried out when a second climax racked her body.

She was incredible. And he wanted her more than he'd
wanted any woman in a very long time. As he drew away
only long enough to shed his briefs and don protection, he
thanked the gods that had allowed their paths to cross and
cursed the fates that had decreed they would only have this
night.

When he lowered himself over her, his whole body was
trembling with the anticipation of finally joining with hers.

She reached for him, her hands linking behind his head, drawing him down for another kiss.

His hands stroked over her again, arousing her, arousing himself. He could feel the blood pounding in his veins, hot and demanding. He could hear the beat of his heart, fast and fierce. Did she know how desperately he wanted her? How he ached for her?

Maybe she did, because her eyes—those gorgeous green eyes—met his and her hips lifted, and the silent urging snapped the last of his self-restraint. He guided himself into the slick heat between her thighs. But despite her apparent readiness, his entry wasn't easy. He gritted his teeth and fisted his hands in the quilt, forcing himself to go slow, to give her time to adjust to his size. His muscles ached with the effort of holding back and his heart pounded against his ribs as he inched a little farther, swallowing her soft sighs of acceptance, of pleasure.

He frowned when he felt an unexpected resistance, but before he could begin to comprehend what it might mean, her legs lifted to lock behind his hips, pulling him deeper so that he pushed through the barrier of her innocence.

He held himself completely still over her, his arms locked in position, his brows drawn together behind his mask.

How was this possible? How could he not have known? And what was he supposed to do now?

But she seemed oblivious to his inner turmoil. Her legs were still hooked around his hips and her hands clutched at his shoulders as she instinctively moved against him, until his control finally snapped and there was nothing left to hold him back.

He drove into her, hard and deep. She cried out, but he recognized that the sound wasn't one of shock or fear but pleasure. She met his rhythm, thrust for thrust, in a primitive and almost desperate race toward the release they both craved.

When the next climax took her to the edge and finally over, he could do nothing but surrender with her.

It was a long time before Marissa managed to catch her breath. She felt stunned, overwhelmed and exhilarated. She'd never even imagined that so many emotions and sensations could rocket through her system at the same time.

She'd felt desire before, subtle tugs that had piqued her curiosity and made her wonder. But there had been absolutely nothing subtle about what she'd experienced in Jupiter's arms. It had been so much more than she'd anticipated, so much more than she ever could have hoped for, and she would always be grateful to him for this night.

Unfortunately, she could tell that he wasn't feeling grateful. He was angry, and she was afraid that she knew why.

"You were a virgin," he said.

The accusation in his tone confirmed her fears and took some of the shine off of the experience for her. She shifted away from him, pulling up the corner of the quilt to cover herself.

"And you wanted someone with more experience?" she guessed, her cheeks flushed with embarrassment.

"I wanted to know." He rose from the bed and paced across the carpet, apparently unconcerned by his own nakedness. When he faced her again, his anger was visible despite the mask he still wore. "I had a right to know."

She pushed herself off of the bed, dragging the cover with her. "I'm sorry you were disappointed."

She started to gather up her costume, but it was hard to see through the tears that blurred her eyes. She'd had the most amazing, exhilarating sexual experience of her life, and her partner wished it had never happened.

He crossed the room in three quick strides and caught her arms. "I wasn't disappointed."

She couldn't read his mood. He'd sounded furious, but now he was looking at her with such tenderness in the depths of those beautiful dark eyes. She wished, for just a moment, that she could push the mask off of his face, to really see this man for who he was. But that wasn't just a futile wish, it was a dangerous one. It was the assurance of anonymity that had given her the courage to follow through with her plan. She couldn't let him discover her identity now.

"But you're angry," she said again.

"At myself."

"I don't understand," she admitted.

"I should have realized." Sighing, he thrust a hand through his hair. "If I'd known, I would have been more careful."

"You didn't hurt me."

But Dante knew that he had. Every muscle in her body had tensed when he'd pushed through the barrier of her virginity. He'd been stunned by the knowledge, and appalled that even when his brain had finally registered that she'd been an innocent, he hadn't been able to stop.

He'd wanted her with such desperation that even knowing she'd been untouched hadn't tempered his desire. In fact, discovering that he was her first had somehow stoked the burning need to take, to claim, to possess. One thought had echoed in his mind: *mine*.

Of course, she couldn't be. Not for more than this one night.

It was something they both knew, though neither had spoken aloud of the fact. The anonymity had served his own purposes—he'd thought this night would be one final fling without the heavy cloak of royal responsibilities that had settled around his shoulders. But now he was ashamed, knowing that he'd taken the innocence of a woman and he didn't even know her name.

He brushed his knuckles gently down her cheek. "Actually, if I'd known you were untouched, I would have made sure you stayed that way."

"Why?"

"Because your first time shouldn't have been with a stranger."

"It was what I wanted," she insisted.

"You deserved better. You deserved more. And I can't give you anything more than this night." His words were heavy with genuine regret.

She lifted her chin. "All of this night?"

It was more of a challenge than a question, and he fought against a smile. She had spirit and spunk and a willingness to go after what she wanted, and he felt both honored and humbled that she'd wanted him.

"Did you think I was going to turn you out of my room now that I've had my way with you?" he asked lightly.

"How would I know? This is new territory for me," she reminded him.

He took the gown that she'd twisted into a ball and set it aside. "I would very much like you to stay."

Marissa thought those words meant that he wanted to take her back to bed. Instead, he excused himself and disappeared into the adjoining bathroom. A few minutes later, he was leading her toward a deep tub filled with fragrant bubbles and surrounded by dozens of flickering candles.

"I thought a bath might help ease some of the soreness in your muscles," he told her.

"I won't be sorry to have aches to remind me of this night," she said, and meant it. "But how can I refuse when you went to so much trouble?"

He smiled and brushed a soft kiss over her lips. "Take as much time as you want."

She didn't plan to be long. She didn't want to waste a

single minute of the short time they would have together, but the bath was too tempting to resist. There was a robe on the back of the door, and she used the belt from it to tie the heavy length of hair up off of her neck. She didn't dare take off the wig or her mask. Though she kept a fairly low profile, there was always the possibility that she might be recognized, and that was a chance she couldn't take. Not tonight.

Pushing the worry aside, she stepped into the tub, sighing as she sank into the warm, scented water. She hadn't realized she was tense until she felt the stiffness seep out of her muscles. But while her body relaxed, her mind raced.

She'd lucked out tonight, she realized that. In retrospect, she could appreciate that her plan to go to bed with a stranger had been not just desperate but reckless. And she had absolutely no regrets. Maybe she did wish that she knew something about the man who had been such an attentive and considerate lover, but there was no point in getting to know a man whose presence in her life couldn't be anything more than temporary.

Pushing those thoughts from her mind, she rose from the tub and briskly rubbed a thick towel over her body. Then she released the tie that was holding her hair, tucked it through the loops of the robe she'd wrapped around herself and stepped back into the bedroom.

He'd lit more candles in here, too, she realized, and folded back the covers on the bed. An antique serving cart had been rolled into the room, on top of which sat an assortment of bowls and platters offering fresh fruits and an assortment of crackers and meats and cheeses. There was also a bottle of champagne in a silver bucket filled with ice beside two crystal flutes waiting to be filled.

"I thought we might have that champagne now," he said.

She was as surprised as she was flattered that he'd gone to so much trouble, but the wild pounding of her heart made her wary. Was she a complete sucker for romantic gestures? Or was it somehow possible that she could be falling in love with a man she didn't even know—a man that she wouldn't ever see again after this night?

She wasn't sure she could answer those questions, or that she wanted to, so she responded to his suggestion instead.

"Champagne sounds wonderful." Then she went to him and linked her hands behind his neck, urging his head down so that she could meet his lips with her own. "Later."

Her heart gave another sigh when he lifted her into his arms and carried her to the bed. She had never dreamed that such romance could be found anywhere outside of the pages of a Victorian novel, and knowing that she was unlikely to experience anything like it again, she savored every moment.

She promised herself that she would remember each stroke of his hands, every touch of his lips, and she knew that she would treasure the memories forever. Whatever happened tomorrow, whatever trials and tribulations she might face in the future, she would always have her recollection of this incredible night. No one could ever take that from her.

He lowered her gently onto the mattress and sank down beside her. He'd shown her pleasure already—so much more than she'd expected. But now, with every brush of his fingertips, there was even more. With every caress, he showed her that she wasn't just desired but revered. With every kiss, he proved that she wasn't just wanted but cherished. And when he finally joined his body with hers again, she felt not just connected but complete.

It was hours later before Marissa finally slipped from his bed.

She hadn't intended to stay so long. Truthfully, her plan for the evening had been remarkably sparse on details beyond finding a willing lover. She knew that she'd been fortunate to find one not just willing but eager to please, and she'd been reluctant to leave the warm comfort of his arms. But she did so, anyway, understanding that she had no other choice.

If anyone was to see her leaving his room—well, she didn't even want to imagine what kind of scandal that would cause. Definitely enough of a scandal that Anthony Volpini would have to accept she would never be his virgin bride. That thought made her smile, and for a brief moment she actually considered stomping her feet as she made her way down the hall so that she would be discovered.

But aside from an arranged marriage to the Duke of Bellemoro, there was nothing Marissa dreaded more than the possibility of finding herself at the center of a media circus. So instead of stomping, she carried her sandals in her hand to ensure a quiet escape as she slipped away from Jupiter's room.

Although she'd stayed longer than she'd intended, it was still early enough that Marissa didn't expect to encounter any servants moving through the halls just yet. So she didn't notice the shadow behind the curtains across the hall or hear the barely audible click of the shutter as her clandestine departure was captured by the camera's lens.

She was gone when Dante awoke. The only proof he had that she'd even been there was a lingering trace of her scent on his pillow and a broken peacock feather that he picked up off of the carpet near the bed.

He sat on the edge of the mattress with the feather in his hand and thought about the woman he knew only as Juno. They'd shared intimacies but not names, and while he didn't regret a minute of the time they'd spent together, he did regret that she'd disappeared from his bed and his life without even saying goodbye.

It wasn't impossible to imagine that their paths might

someday cross again, but the possibility did nothing to ease the unexpected emptiness inside of him. Because he knew that, in the unlikely event that they did meet again, he wouldn't recognize her. If he really wanted to ascertain her identity, he could probably finagle a copy of the guest list from one of the palace staff. But then what?

Was he really prepared to track down every female guest until he found a green-eyed redhead with a sexy little mole on her right hip? Of course not, because even if he had the time or the energy for such an endeavor, the discovery of Juno's true identity would change nothing. He'd known when he invited her back to his room that they could never be anything more than strangers in the night.

So why was he wishing for something different now? Why was he fantasizing about an impossible reunion with a woman he didn't even know?

His future was already laid out for him and last night had been only a temporary and forbidden deviation from the path that had been set for him at birth. It was time to set himself back on that path and be the king his country needed.

It was time to meet his bride.

Chapter Three

Marissa slapped a hand on her alarm to silence the incessant buzzing. She wasn't ready to get out of bed. Her reluctance had nothing to do with the fact that she'd crawled between the sheets less than four hours earlier and everything to do with the incredible sensual dreams from which she never wanted to awaken.

Dreams of a mouthwateringly sexy god with fathomless dark eyes behind a gold mask, a strong jaw with just a hint of shadow and a mouth that was both elegantly shaped and infinitely talented. She could almost taste his kiss, dark and potent and thoroughly intoxicating.

She snuggled deeper under the covers, certain she could feel the heat of his skin beneath her palms as she explored the planes and angles of all those glorious muscles. Broad shoulders, strong pecs, rippling abs and a very impressive—

She slapped at the alarm again.

Then, with a sigh that was equal parts resignation and

regret, she hit the off button and eased herself into sitting position.

Pushing back the covers, she swung her legs over the edge of the mattress. She winced a little as she made her way to the bathroom, feeling the tug of strained muscles in her thighs, the ache in her shoulders and an unfamiliar tenderness in her breasts.

Not a dream, after all, she realized, smiling as she turned on the shower and stripped away the silk boxers and cami that she slept in. Memories of the previous night played through her mind as she stepped beneath the spray.

A fantasy come true, but definitely not a dream.

As she'd donned her costume in preparation of the ball the previous evening, she'd worried that she might regret embarking on her course of action, but she'd been more worried about what her future might hold if she chose a course of inaction.

She'd taken control of her life and her future—as much as she could, anyway. Because according to the outdated but still valid laws of the principality, Marissa *could* be forced to marry the duke, but at least she wouldn't go to his bed a virgin on her wedding night.

She'd evaluated her options and she'd made a choice, and she didn't regret it now. How could she regret what had been the most incredible experience of her entire life?

If she felt any disappointment, it was only because she might never again know the kind of pleasure Jupiter had given to her. He'd been an incredibly attentive lover. He'd not just touched but tantalized every inch of her body with his hands and his lips and his tongue—

She turned her face into the spray and nudged the temperature dial downward to help cool her heated skin and resolved to stop fantasizing about what was past.

After she'd stepped out of the shower and toweled off, she

opened her closet in search of an appropriate outfit for brunch with her mother. In the midst of various shades of ivory and cream and beige, the stunningly vibrant dress she'd worn the night before shone like a beacon. Instinctively her hand reached out, her fingers caressing the shimmery fabric, and she made a mental note to send a heartfelt thank-you card to her dressmaker.

Then she purposely moved Juno's dress to the back of the closet because she was no longer a Roman goddess. She was just an ordinary princess again and she had to look the part for her meeting with the Princess Royal.

She selected a simple beige-and-white sheath-style dress, slipped her feet into a pair of matching kitten heels, then brushed her hair away from her face and secured it in a knot at the back of her head. She added simple gold hoop earrings and a couple of gold bangles on her wrist and decided the overall look was stylish if rather bland—and perfectly suited to Princess Marissa.

You're even more beautiful than I anticipated.

The echo of Jupiter's reverent whisper made her heart sigh. He'd made her feel beautiful. Desirable. *Desired.* But there was no hint of that woman in the reflection that looked back at her now.

She turned away from the mirror, refusing to admit that she longed to feel that way again. She knew that she could be beautiful. Elena had been—and still was—a stunning woman, and many people had remarked upon the similarities between mother and daughter. But while the Princess Royal always took care to highlight her best features, Marissa chose to downplay her own. Beautiful women did not go unnoticed, and she preferred the freedom to live her life as she chose rather than under a microscope.

Of course, she was a princess, so a certain amount of media attention was unavoidable. She even courted that attention when it served her purposes. But most of the time, she was happy to let the paparazzi chase after those who were much more bold and beautiful.

A knock at the door jolted her out of her reverie. She set down the cup of coffee she'd just poured and went to answer the summons.

There were few people who could gain access to the private elevator leading to her tenth-floor condo, so she wasn't surprised to open the door and find both of her sisters-in-law on the other side. She was disappointed that they didn't have her nieces with them, as she absolutely doted on Michael's five-year-old Riley and Cameron's eleven-month-old Jaedyn.

"What are you doing here?" she asked, because she knew they didn't have any plans to get together this morning.

Michael's wife, Hannah, was the first to respond. "We were worried about you."

Marissa led the way to the kitchen, where she filled another mug with coffee and a third with only milk. "Why would you be worried?"

"Because you had a migraine severe enough to keep you at home last night. It's not like you to miss an event benefiting the Children's Hospital," Gabriella—Cameron's very expectant wife—explained, accepting the milk with more resignation than enthusiasm.

She'd forgotten the excuse she'd made to both of them to explain her supposed absence from the event the night before. Though she didn't lie easily or well, the fib had been necessary to ensure that they weren't looking for her in the crowd.

Hannah stirred a spoonful of sugar into her coffee. "I called last night to see if you needed anything, but when there was no answer, I figured you turned off the ringer because of the headache."

Gabby's gaze narrowed suspiciously. "But when Hannah

told me that she'd called and didn't get an answer, I began to suspect that maybe you didn't miss the ball at all."

She sipped her coffee. "You're right. I was there," Marissa admitted. "But I left early."

"With the sexy guy in the purple toga?"

Marissa didn't bother to deny it. She'd already proven that she couldn't lie to them—at least not very well—and she didn't want to, anyway. They weren't just her sisters-in-law, they were her best friends, and she desperately needed friends to confide in right now.

"With Jupiter," she confirmed.

Gabby grinned. "Good for you."

Hannah's head swiveled toward her. "Are you kidding? It's not good—it's crazy."

"Was it good?" Gabby asked, not the least bit chastened by Hannah's outrage.

Marissa couldn't help but smile. "It was…fabulous."

"Details," Gabby immediately demanded.

Hannah only sighed.

"I'm sorry if you're disappointed in me," Marissa said to Michael's wife, and meant it.

"I'm not disappointed in you, just surprised," Hannah told her. "I've never known you to be reckless or impulsive, and leaving the ball with a stranger—"

"Was necessary," she interjected.

Even Gabriella seemed surprised by that revelation. "Why?"

Marissa lifted her chin. "Because I'd decided it was finally time to lose my virginity."

Her brothers' wives exchanged another look. Obviously neither of them had been aware of her lack of sexual experience, and why would they be?

"Okay, back up a minute and put this in context for us," Hannah suggested. "Why, having made it to this point in your life without losing your virginity, was it suddenly so urgent to do so?"

"Because there are rumors floating around that the Duke of Bellemoro is in the market for his second wife and, based on several appointments that he's had with the Princess Royal over the past few weeks, I figured out that Elena was preparing to offer me as a virgin sacrifice."

"There aren't a lot of suitable marriage prospects for a bona fide princess," Hannah noted. "So I can see why your mother might consider a match with someone holding such a high hereditary title to be a coup."

"But the Duke of Bellemoro?" Gabby winced sympathetically. She, too, had obviously heard the rumors of the duke's sexual proclivities. And despite his appreciation for women with a multitude of experience in his bedroom, he'd let it be known that he was seeking a more innocent type for his bride.

"Which is why I decided that I wasn't going to be manipulated," Marissa said firmly. "Not anymore."

"So don't be," Gabby said. "It's not as if Elena can force you to marry against your will."

"Actually, she can," Hannah interjected, sounding almost apologetic. "Archaic as it may be, the laws of this country still allow the parents of a princess to enter into a legal contract of marriage on her behalf."

"But not the parents of a prince?" Gabriella was as incensed by the inequality of its application as the law itself.

"I said it was archaic," Hannah reminded her.

"It's an old and acceptable tradition," Marissa said. "And my mother knows that I would honor such a contract because it's my duty as a member of the royal family to respect our history and uphold our customs."

"Because you'd never do anything that might create a scandal," Gabby noted.

"Losing your virginity to a stranger seems pretty scandalous to me," Hannah said.

"If the Princess Royal's daughter lost her virginity to a stranger, it would be scandalous," Marissa acknowledged, which was why she'd been so worried about the possibility that someone might recognize her. And during one turn around the dance floor, she'd spotted her sisters-in-law on the perimeter and had felt the weight of Gabriella's gaze on her. But her brother's wife had shown no hint of recognition, which reassured Marissa that her true identity would not be discovered. "Which is why I made sure that no one would know that I was Juno."

"Gabby recognized you," Hannah pointed out.

"I suspected," she clarified. "And I should say now that you looked absolutely stunning."

Before Marissa could respond, Hannah forged ahead again.

"It was still a crazy idea. No, not just crazy but dangerous," she said. "Do you have any idea how many things could have gone wrong?"

"Nothing went wrong," Marissa told her.

"Nothing except that you slept with a man you don't even know," Hannah countered.

"Actually, I didn't sleep at all until I got home around three this morning."

Gabby grinned. "You're actually bragging."

Marissa lifted her chin. Maybe she was bragging, and she wasn't going to apologize for it. If a wedding to the Duke of Bellemoro was in her future, at least she would have the memories of one fabulous night to help get her through it.

Hannah looked at her, the furrow in her brow easing. "It really was good?"

"It really was fabulous," she said again.

"Well, I guess that's something," she relented. "But you should have at least asked his name."

"I couldn't," Marissa said. "Because I had no intention of telling him mine. I wanted to be anonymous so that, for the first time in my life, I could feel confident that a man was interested in me and not my title or political connections."

"Still, I would think you'd at least be curious about his true identity," Gabriella mused.

"Of course I am. But the whole point of putting my plan into action last night was to ensure that no one would know who I was—it would hardly be fair if I changed the rules now."

"It would be easy enough to track him down," Hannah told her. "All you'd have to do is contact the palace's master of the household and find out who was staying in…whatever room he was staying in."

"It was the corner suite," Marissa answered automatically, "but I'm not going to do it."

"Why not?" Gabby demanded, clearly disappointed.

"Because he obviously had his own reasons for wanting to remain anonymous."

"Which only makes me more curious."

"Maybe he's married," Hannah suggested.

"He's not," Marissa assured her. "I did ask about that."

"Glad to know you did exercise some moral judgment before you gave your virginity to a stranger," Hannah noted, tongue-in-cheek.

"Thank you," Marissa said. "Now, if you two are finished with your interrogation, I'm going to kick you out so that I can stop at the hospital before I have to meet my mother and potential suitor for brunch."

Gabriella paused in the act of pushing back her chair. "Why did you say 'potential suitor'?"

"Just repeating Elena's words," Marissa explained. "You know my mother thrives on mystery and drama."

"So she never actually said it was the Duke of Bellemoro?" Hannah asked.

"No," she admitted, still not following the direction of their parallel thinking.

"What if it's not the duke?" Gabby pressed.

Marissa dismissed the possibility with a shake of her head. "Who else could it be?"

Dante had first met the Princess Royal about half a dozen years earlier when he'd accompanied his father on an official visit to Tesoro del Mar. His initial impression had been of a woman whose beauty was surpassed only by her ambition—an impression that was confirmed when, a few weeks after he'd taken the throne, she contacted him with a proposal to strengthen the bond between their respective countries.

At the time, he'd had more pressing issues to contend with, and she'd graciously agreed to defer the matter to another time. But when the invitation to the Mythos Ball arrived in the mail, he'd accepted that this meeting was one that could be put off no longer.

Since assuming his new role, Dante had been the recipient of more marriage proposals than he wanted to count. The majority of them were personal entreaties sent by hopeful future queens, though some were sent on behalf of the potential brides-to-be by a mother or sister or grandmother. Dante had delegated the task of responding to these offers to the palace's junior secretaries.

Elena's letter had been the exception. He was all too aware that Ardena's relationship with Tesoro del Mar—her closest neighbor, naval ally and trading partner—had become strained in recent years. Just as he was aware that it was his responsibility to do whatever he could to rectify the situation.

A marriage between Ardena's king and a Tesorian princess would go a long way toward doing that.

When he arrived at Elena's estate, Dante was prepared for the Princess Royal to do or say almost anything to convince him that he should marry her daughter, and he was willing to let himself be convinced. As his father had pointed out to him, there weren't a lot of single women of appropriate genealogy—and even fewer still with whom he didn't already have some kind of history.

"Your Majesty." The Princess Royal curtsied. "I'm so pleased you were able to take this time to meet with me while you're visiting Tesoro del Mar."

He bowed to her in turn. "The pleasure is mine, Your Highness."

"I trust you had a good time at the ball last evening," she said when they were seated in the parlor.

"I did," he agreed, though the remark caused his mind to flash back not to the charity event but to the pleasures he'd enjoyed after leaving the ballroom.

"Marissa will be pleased to hear it." Elena passed him a delicate gold-rimmed cup. "Unfortunately, she wasn't able to be there last night, but she tries to ensure that the annual ball isn't just successful but also enjoyable."

"I've heard that she's very committed to her work at the hospital." He sipped his coffee.

"She has experience with numerous charitable endeavors—an essential attribute for the wife of a king."

Dante had always found it easier to negotiate with people who were forthright about their demands rather than those who tiptoed around them. It was clear that the Princess Royal didn't believe in tiptoeing.

"I don't disagree," he told her. "But there are many other factors to consider."

"You won't find another candidate more suitable than Princess Marissa," Elena promised. "She has lived her whole life with the demands and duties of royal life, she is educated, well mannered, kindhearted and still innocent."

Definitely no tiptoeing going on here.

Dante set down his cup and cleared his throat. "I do think that the criteria for suitability have changed somewhat with the times."

"But your country's Marriage Act still enumerates some very specific criteria," Elena pointed out. "Including that the bride of a king must be of noble birth and pure virtue."

Technically, she was correct. But since a king was entitled to privacy on his wedding night, he wasn't concerned about the latter stipulation. "I'm not sure that's a realistic expectation in this day and age," he acknowledged, refusing to think about his mysterious virgin lover of the previous evening. "I'm more concerned that my future bride is untouched by scandal."

"I assure you that my daughter is untouched in every way that matters."

He forced a smile, though the calculation in her eyes made him uneasy. It was obvious that the Princess Royal wanted a union between their families and would do everything in her power to make it happen, and he couldn't help but feel a tug of sympathy for the princess whose mother so clearly viewed her as a commodity to be bartered.

"You don't think she would be reluctant to leave her friends and family here to live in another country?"

"Ardena is not so far," Elena said dismissively. "And a marriage between its king and a Tesorian princess would only strengthen the historically close ties between our two countries. It might even help our people forget the unnecessary stir created by your father on his last visit."

"Whether the stir was or was not necessary is a matter of perspective," Dante retorted, not even attempting to disguise the edge in his tone. "And he had reason to be concerned about your son's relationship with my sister."

"Well, that's past history, anyway," she said, conveniently forgetting that she'd been the one to bring up the subject. "What matters now is the future."

"Agreed," he said, only because he knew that the relationship between Prince Cameron and Princess Leticia alleged in the newspaper headlines had been predicated on nothing more than one dance in a nightclub.

Of course, the relationship Elena was advocating for her daughter would be based on even less, and Dante couldn't help wondering if the princess in question might not want more than a marriage founded solely on politics. And he was both baffled and infuriated that her mother didn't seem to want more for her.

Or maybe he was angry that he wasn't allowed to want more for himself. His parents' marriage had been "suggested" rather than arranged, and they'd been lucky enough to fall in love so that they wanted to honor the wishes of their respective families. When Dante had protested that he should be given the opportunity to find love, too, his parents had bluntly pointed out that he'd managed to find enough lovers without worrying about emotional attachments, and now it was time for him to accept that he had a responsibility to his country and its people. And that responsibility took precedence over all else.

"How does Princess Marissa feel about a potential wedding to the king of Ardena?"

"You don't need to worry about her feelings," she assured him. "She understands very well that duty must come before desire."

"You seem certain of that," he noted.

"Marissa understands the demands and responsibilities of

your position. She will stand by your side when you need her there and remain in the background when you don't."

He wasn't sure he wanted a wife who would be so docile and unassuming. He'd always admired women who had their own thoughts and ambitions, who challenged him to consider different ideas and perspectives, who were intelligent and strong and passionate. He wanted passion.

He wanted Juno.

He pushed the haunting memories of the previous night from his mind. He'd acted impulsively and recklessly, and he knew it couldn't ever happen again. He was the king of Ardena now, and he needed to find a wife.

He, too, knew that duty must come before desire, and he accepted that there could be no more stolen moments with sexy strangers. So he directed his attention back to his hostess.

"When can I meet your daughter?" he asked.

The Princess Royal's smile was smug. "She will join us for brunch."

Chapter Four

When her mother scheduled brunch for one o'clock, Marissa knew that the meal would be on the table at one o'clock—the Princess Royal was absolutely unyielding when it came to maintaining her schedule. Marissa also knew that Elena would not be pleased by her daughter's arrival at 1:08.

It wouldn't matter that she had called as she was leaving the hospital to advise that she was running late. The Princess Royal was as intolerant of excuses as she was of tardiness.

Marissa realized her lateness wouldn't score any points with the duke, either, but she was less concerned about him. Or maybe she was hoping that Anthony Volpini would be so annoyed by her delay that he would abandon all thoughts of marrying her. Buoyed by this thought, she practically skipped up the steps to her mother's front door.

Edmond, her mother's butler, had obviously been watching for her, because he opened the door before Marissa even had a chance to ring the bell.

"The Princess Royal and the king are in the dining room."

She started to nod, accepting that her mother wouldn't wait even eight minutes for an expected guest, then froze when the import of his words registered. "The king?"

"His Majesty, Dante Romero, King of Ardena," Edmond announced formally.

"But I thought…"

It didn't matter what she'd thought. Certainly her mother's butler wasn't interested in hearing about her mistaken assumptions. Marissa drew in a deep breath as she tried to consider the implications of this revelation, but she could only think, *I'm going to meet the king of Ardena*—a thought that made her heart beat hard and fast.

With excitement? Or apprehension? She honestly didn't know because she didn't know a lot about him. Although Dante Romero had been a favorite subject of many tabloids for a lot of years, Marissa had never paid much attention to those reports. But when he'd assumed the throne in February—after health issues forced his father to step down—it had become all but impossible to open up a newspaper or turn on a television and not see a photo or a video clip. And she had to admit, it was never a hardship to look at his picture.

But while the tabloids had loved him because the escapades of a playboy prince always generated good headlines, the legitimate press had been much more critical. Especially since he'd transitioned from "the Crown Prince of Ardena" to "His Majesty the King." They criticized his experience, challenged his knowledge of laws and customs, and questioned his ability to relate to his subjects. But he'd apparently put in a lot of long hours and made a concerted effort to alleviate the concerns of his detractors, and if he'd made a few mistakes along the way, Marissa thought those mistakes only proved that even a king was human.

That thought helped steady her erratically beating heart.

Still, she wished her mother had given her some warning. But the Princess Royal always liked to have the upper hand, and she obviously had it now since she'd somehow convinced the king to come to Tesoro del Mar to meet her daughter.

Elena had commented often enough that a princess's options for a good marriage were limited, and Marissa didn't doubt that she would have happily given her consent to any noble who requested her daughter's hand. But if Marissa somehow managed to snag the interest of a king...

Unfortunately, she knew that the king wasn't really interested in her. How could he be when he'd never even met her? Besides, she wasn't a cover model or a famous opera singer or a Hollywood starlet—and yes, the king had dated each of those and a lot more famous and beautiful women—but she *was* of noble birth. No, the reason for the king's presence in Tesoro del Mar had nothing to do with her personally and everything to do with politics.

"Are you all right, Your Highness?"

"Actually, I'm famished," she responded to the butler's question.

He smiled. "Cook has kept your plate warm. I'll make sure it's brought in right away."

"Thank you, Edmond." Marissa smiled back, then hurried to the dining room, now twelve minutes late.

Dante recognized her the moment she walked through the door.

Although they'd never met, she looked just like she did in the photos he'd uncovered—and very much a princess.

She wasn't the type of woman who would ordinarily attract his attention, even in a crowd of one, but he reminded himself that he wasn't just looking for a wife for himself but a queen for his country. And there was no doubt that Princess Marissa had all the grace and poise required of a woman in that position. She also had excellent bone structure, flawless skin and long, dark hair that he thought might be more flattering if it was left loose to frame her face rather than scraped back into a tight knot at the base of her neck.

And though he would never claim to be an expert on fashion, he felt her wardrobe could use some work, too. In every picture he'd seen of her, she was wearing some shade of beige. The dress she was wearing today was no different. It was stylish enough, he imagined, but the boxy cut gave no hint of any feminine curves and the beige-and-white combination was beyond bland, making him wonder if she had some kind of moral objection to color.

He tucked away the thought and pushed back his chair when she stepped into the room. The movement caught her attention, and her gaze shifted in his direction.

Their eyes locked, and Dante was surprised to realize that her eyes weren't brown, as he'd believed, but the color of amber, fringed by long, dark lashes.

The second surprise was the tightening in his gut, raw and purely sexual, and an inexplicable sense of recognition.

"Your Majesty," she said, dipping into an elegant curtsy. "I apologize if I've kept you waiting."

He bowed. "No apology is necessary," he assured her, though the disapproval in Elena's gaze warned that she did not agree. "I'm just pleased that you are able to join us."

The princess lowered herself into the chair that the butler held for her. As soon as she was seated, a server appeared with her plate.

"The king was telling me about the sights he'd like to see while he's in Tesoro del Mar," Elena said to her daughter.

Her intention might have been to simply make the princess aware of the topic of conversation, but the subtle edge in her voice gave Dante the impression that Elena was making a point about her daughter's tardiness rather than the current discussion.

Marissa's only response was to ask him, "Are you here on vacation, Your Majesty?"

"This trip is a combination of business and pleasure," he told her. "Although I'm hoping it will be less of the former and more of the latter."

"And are you enjoying yourself so far?" She picked up her knife and fork and sliced off the end of a crepe.

"Always," he assured her. "It is a beautiful country—in many ways so much like my own, and in many ways different."

"I've never been to Ardena," the princess admitted.

"Then you should definitely visit," he said. "And when you do, I'd be honored to have you stay at the palace as my guest."

"That sounds like a marvelous idea," the Princess Royal declared.

Marissa's smile was much more tentative than her mother's response.

"In the meantime," Dante continued, "I was hoping you might have some time tomorrow afternoon to attend the hot-air-balloon festival at Falcon Ridge with me."

"I appreciate the invitation," the princess said graciously, "but I have plans with my niece tomorrow."

Elena's eyes were frigid when she looked across the table at her daughter. "King Dante has invited you to spend the day with him," she admonished.

Marissa met her mother's gaze evenly, suggesting to Dante that she might not be as docile and dutiful as the Princess Royal had implied—a possibility that intrigued him.

He'd never felt the need to surround himself with people who would agree with his every word and deed, and he'd never enjoyed being with a woman who couldn't express her own thoughts and feelings. He was pleased by this evidence that the Princess Royal's daughter would not be one of them.

"And I have a previous commitment," Marissa pointed out to her mother.

"Which I wouldn't expect you to break," he assured her. "But maybe your niece would enjoy attending the festival with us."

Marissa's attention shifted back to him, revealing both surprise and suspicion. But when she spoke, her voice was carefully neutral. "That sounds like fun—if you're sure you wouldn't mind spending the afternoon with a five-year-old."

"I'm sure it will be my pleasure," he countered.

Apparently satisfied with the progress that had been made, the Princess Royal monopolized the rest of the conversation as they finished brunch. Marissa managed to eat a few bites of crepe and a couple of pieces of fruit, but her stomach was too tied up in knots to attempt any more than that. She didn't doubt for a minute that her mother had been the one to set up this meeting with the sole purpose of putting Marissa on display in front of the king, but the fact that he was here, having brunch in Elena's dining room, proved that he was at least considering the potential benefits of a union between their families.

And while the possibility of marrying the king of Ardena didn't fill her with the same kind of panic she'd experienced at the thought of spending the rest of her life with the Duke of Bellemoro, it didn't fill her with joy, either. Because whether she was compelled to marry the duke or the king or anyone else, it was the obligation aspect that made her uneasy. She wanted to fall in love and get married for all the right reasons, but she was a princess, and she understood her duty.

She was relieved when her mother stood up, signaling an end to the brunch. The king graciously thanked Elena for "the exquisite meal and delightful company" and formally bowed over her hand as an indication that he was taking his leave. He then turned to Marissa and bowed again as he raised her hand to brush his lips to the back of it.

Marissa held herself still, refusing to give any outward indication of the shocks and jolts that ricocheted through her body. She recognized the kiss for what it was—nothing more than an habitual gesture. She'd had her hand kissed before and the king had, no doubt, kissed countless women's hands in a similar fashion. There was certainly nothing provocative or even flirtatious about the gesture, and yet the brief touch of his mouth on her skin made her feel all hot and tingly.

She'd had the same kind of visceral reaction only once before, and that had been as recently as last night. The realization made her uneasy. Was it possible that having sex once—well, actually, three times over the course of one night—could turn her into a wanton? She was ashamed to think it might be true, but what other explanation could there be for her immediate physical response to a man she didn't even know?

Or maybe she was just shallow enough to be turned on by a handsome face. Because there was no denying that Dante Romero was far more handsome than any other man she'd ever met, and even more than she'd expected. He had a strong jaw, bedroom eyes and a sexy mouth—any one of those features alone would have snagged a woman's attention, but put them all together and the effect was irresistible.

As if the gods hadn't blessed him enough with that face, they'd also given him more than six feet in height and filled all of those inches with long, lean muscles. He was, without a doubt, the complete package—and judging from the glint in those dark eyes, the hint of a smile that played at the corners of those sexy lips, and too many headlines to count, he knew it.

"I'm already looking forward to tomorrow," he told her.

And since he knew it, she didn't see any need to cater to his undoubtedly oversize ego. She ensured that her response was polite but cool, giving no hint of the heat that was running through her veins. "As am I, Your Majesty."

Elena waited until the king had exited the room before facing her. "What was that about?" she demanded.

For a minute, Marissa thought the Princess Royal had somehow been privy to the lustful desires pulsing in her blood. But when her mother spoke again, Marissa realized that she hadn't picked up on any undercurrents between her daughter and the king.

"I went to great lengths to bring the king here to meet you—the least you could have done was show some genuine interest and appreciation."

"If you wanted me to be gracious and charming, you might have given me some warning," Marissa told her.

"I didn't want to get your hopes up, in case the arrangements for his trip fell through."

"That was thoughtful," Marissa said, "but unnecessary, because I don't have any hopes."

"Don't you even think about sabotaging this," Elena warned in an icy tone.

"Why would I? If you don't manage to finalize an agreement with the king, I'll just become a pawn in your negotiations with someone else."

"You should be flattered that the king of Ardena is interested."

"And I would be, if his interest was based on anything more than strengthening ties between two countries."

"Dante Romero is one of the most sought-after bachelors in the world."

"Who probably has a mistress in every major city around the globe," Marissa noted.

Elena shrugged as if the possibility was of no concern. "But he'll only have one wife, and that wife could be you."

"I've agreed to go to Falcon Ridge with him tomorrow and I will, but you're deluding yourself if you think that there will be a proposal at the end of the day," she warned her mother. "The king of Ardena has dated some of the most famous women in the world—models and movie stars and musicians. They're not just beautiful and glamorous, but savvy and sophisticated. Women who can not only handle living in the spotlight, but seek it out. Women who are absolutely nothing like me."

"Those are the women he dated," her mother agreed. "And not a single one of them would make an appropriate queen. You, on the other hand, are exactly what the king is looking for in a bride."

"He told you what he's looking for?"

"The requirements of a royal bride in Ardena aren't a matter of choice but of custom—and your blood is blue and your virtue unquestionable."

Marissa didn't dare correct her misconception. Instead, she only said, "It's still possible that the king might decide we're simply not compatible."

"That's his decision to make, of course." Elena narrowed her gaze. "But I trust you will do everything you can to help him see that you are."

"Why does this matter so much to you? Why do you care who I marry or even if I do?"

"I care because you're my daughter, and because it would be nice if at least one of my children exceeded my expectations."

Finally, Marissa got it. The Princess Royal had once envisioned grand futures for each of her sons. After Prince Julian was killed and his brother, Rowan, had taken the throne, Elena had attempted to undermine the prince regent and install Cameron in the palace. She'd been bitterly disappointed when her efforts failed. She'd been even more frustrated with Michael, because her oldest son had never shown any interest in following any path but his own. But all she'd ever expected of her daughter was that Marissa would marry well—as Elena's own father had expected of her.

Of course, the Princess Royal had defied her father by running off to marry a farmer. Unfortunately, Marissa had no similar prospects. And, in any event, she figured giving her virginity away to a stranger was probably enough defiance for one week. Besides, she didn't think there was any real danger of Ardena's new king actually wanting to marry her, and if keeping him company while he was in Tesoro del Mar kept her mother off of her back, it was a price she was willing to pay.

"I'll do my best to ensure the king has a wonderful time tomorrow," she promised.

"It would be better if you could spend the day alone with him. The presence of a child is hardly conducive to romance."

The "child" in question being Elena's granddaughter and the firstborn child of Marissa's brother Michael. And while there were many responses that sprang to mind, she reminded herself of the dangers of antagonizing her mother and only said, "The king didn't seem to have any objections to including Riley."

"That doesn't make it okay."

"If he wants to see me again after tomorrow, I'll make sure that I'm available," she said, trusting the offer would placate her mother.

"Where are you going now?" Elena demanded as Marissa started for the door.

"Back to the hospital."

"Weren't you already there today? Isn't that why you kept us waiting?"

"Yes," she admitted, though she could have pointed out that no one had, in fact, waited for her. "And I'm truly sorry that I was late but Devon was in respiratory distress and I couldn't leave until I knew that his condition was stabilized."

Of course, her mother didn't know who Devon was, nor did she care enough to ask. She'd never understood Marissa's commitment to Juno's Touch and the babies who passed through its doors.

Her colleagues at the hospital liked to tease that Juno's Touch was Marissa's baby, and in many ways that was true. She'd nurtured the idea from start to finish—an endeavor that had taken a lot more than the nine months of most babies. But it had been, and continued to be, a labor of love.

Of course, she wanted real babies someday. She wanted to experience the awe of growing a child in her womb, the satisfaction of nourishing a baby from her own breast, the completion of knowing she had someone to love forever. But until that time came, she had Juno's Touch, and she happily gave it her heart and soul.

"I'm not sure your continued involvement at the hospital is wise. You get far too attached to babies that aren't even yours," Elena admonished.

Unlike the Princess Royal, who hadn't even tried to form an attachment with her own three children, Marissa thought, though she didn't dare speak the words aloud.

"I can't spend all of my time at spa appointments and social events," she said lightly.

"Speaking of which, you might take some time to have your hair styled and get your nails done before tomorrow."

Marissa touched her lips to her mother's cheek. "I'll see if I can fit that in," she lied and made her escape.

Dante didn't have any specific plans when he left the Princess Royal's house. He only knew that he wasn't ready to go back to the palace and the suite of rooms that haunted him with memories of the hours he'd spent making love with the mysterious Juno the night before. So he instructed the chauffeur to take a drive along the waterfront, and he let his mind wander as he enjoyed the view out of his window.

Tesoro del Mar really was a beautiful country, but as much as he always enjoyed visiting, he always looked forward to going home. This time, he was less eager. Even though he wasn't scheduled to return to Ardena until the end of the following week, he knew that his parents would expect he would be ready to announce that he'd chosen a bride by then. And Dante's reluctance to settle down was exceeded only by his determination not to disappoint them again.

Thinking of home now, he reached inside the pocket of his jacket for his cell phone. Hearing his mother's voice on the other end of the line brought an immediate smile to his lips.

They spoke briefly for a few minutes before he ventured to ask, "How's Dad?"

"Well enough to be in the pool flirting with another woman."

The lightness of her tone eased some of his worry. "How is the physiotherapy going?"

"I thought he should be coming to the end of his treatment schedule, but Rita assures me that he's continuing to make progress. Personally, I think she enjoys the flirting as much as your father does."

"Whatever works," Dante said, echoing the doctor who had forced the king to face some hard truths about his future if he didn't take immediate action to improve his health.

It was the same doctor's advice that had finally convinced Benedicto to step down from the throne. Since then, the former king's blood pressure had leveled out, decreasing the likelihood of any more strokes and increasing the doctor's optimism for his recovery.

"How was the ball?" his mother asked now. "Did you meet Princess Marissa?"

"Good and yes," he responded to her questions in turn.

"And?" she prompted.

"We have a date tomorrow."

"I knew she wouldn't be able to resist you," Arianna said.

"I'm not sure that's the case at all," he confided. "Her mother seems more interested in a potential union than the princess herself."

"I can't say that surprises me," she admitted.

"You know the Princess Royal?"

"Our paths have crossed on a few occasions over the years."

"Why do I get the feeling there's something you're not telling me?"

"There's lots of things I don't tell you," she said without apology. "Because you have more important things to worry about. Including the fact that Dr. Geffen gave the board her resignation today."

Dante swore under his breath.

"She's not the only one we're going to lose if we don't get the hospital redevelopment plan back on schedule," Arianna warned.

"Tell me what I can do to help."

"The fundraising committee has some great ideas for drawing people and money to the auction." There was a momentary pause before she continued. "It was suggested that Princess Marissa's endorsement—and ideally her attendance—would succeed in focusing more attention on the cause."

Because Princess Marissa was famous not just for being royal but for her dedication to ensuring access to quality medical care for all children.

"Then make sure they know that Princess Marissa will be there."

There was another pause as his mother absorbed this information. Then she said, "Don't you think you should talk to Marissa about that first?"

A sign on the edge of the road caught his attention. Beside the familiar blue *H* were the words Port Augustine Children's Hospital.

"I'm on it," Dante promised her and disconnected the call.

Dante didn't actually expect the princess would be at the hospital on a Saturday afternoon, but he thought that if he could find a young female nurse or orderly on a break, he might be able to charm her into giving him a cursory tour of the facility. Except that instead of heading directly to the cafeteria, he followed the signs to the pediatric intensive-care unit first.

Siobhan Breslin had been airlifted from Mercy Medical Center in Ardena to PACH for surgery to repair an atrial septal defect. He'd been informed that the operation was a success, but since Dante was at the hospital, anyway, he thought he would check her status himself.

He found the neonatal intensive care but wasn't sure where to go from there. He thought about asking a nurse to direct him, but recognized that doing so could lead to questions he wasn't prepared to answer. When he caught a glimpse of Fiona, the baby's mom, he decided that Siobhan's condition was being monitored by enough people without his interference.

Making his way down another corridor, he found himself in front of a nursery. The words Juno's Touch were etched in the glass.

His mind automatically shifted from babies to red-haired, green-eyed goddesses and wondered at the irony of fate that the harder he tried to put the mysterious woman out of his mind, the more impossible it seemed. He didn't even know her real name—he didn't know anything about her. It was supposed to have been an interlude, one night in which he forgot about the obligations and responsibilities inherent to his title. One night to make love with a woman who made no demands and had no expectations of him.

His meeting with the Princess Royal and the recent conversation with his mother had clearly reminded him of those expectations, and he resolved to forget about the goddess and focus on the princess.

The sound of heels clicking on the tile floor drew his attention away from the nursery. When he turned, he found himself face-to-face with his future queen.

Chapter Five

The princess dropped into a curtsy, the gesture as elegant as it was automatic.

"I didn't realize you were visiting the hospital today, Your Majesty."

"It was an impulse," he admitted. And though he was just as surprised to see her here, he also recognized that this chance meeting might be the perfect opportunity to gain some insights into her role at the hospital. "But PACH is one of the most renowned children's hospitals in the Mediterranean and I was curious to see what you've done here before we finalize plans for expansion of our pediatric wing."

She scanned the ID tag that was pinned to her dress, releasing the locks on the door that controlled entry and exit to the nursery. "I'd heard that the expansion plans had been put on hold indefinitely."

"Some unexpected budget shortfalls have caused delays, but the plans remain unchanged," he assured her, deliberately downplaying what was yet another unfortunate situation attributed to his rule.

"Then you should definitely take a closer look around," she said. He accepted the invitation by following her through the door.

She went to one of the sinks along the back wall and soaped up her hands. "If you have specific questions, you should talk to Dr. Marotta," she advised. "I don't think he's here today, but I'd be happy to set up an appointment if you wanted to meet with him at another time."

Her offer sounded both genuine and heartfelt, and he was grateful. "Thank you."

She smiled as she rinsed and dried her hands. "We have a wonderful facility here and I'm always happy to show it off."

The princess then took a sterile gown from the cupboard and slipped it on over her dress before moving to one of the bassinets. She said something else, but her voice was pitched so low that he knew her words were intended only for the impossibly tiny baby she lifted into her arms.

"He's a little guy, isn't he?"

"You should have seen him when he was born," Marissa said. "He was just over three pounds then, but he's almost five now and getting bigger and stronger every day."

She scanned her ID tag at another door and Dante followed her into a room decorated in muted tones of blue and green with thick sage-colored carpet. There were prints on the walls—copies of famous works by Sisley and Pissarro and Monet—and classical music playing softly in the background. About a dozen rocking chairs were set up around the perimeter of the room, interspersed with tables offering books and magazines.

The princess then settled into a chair near the door and gestured for him to take the one beside her.

On the far side of the room, he saw a white-haired grandmother rocking a baby wrapped in a pink blanket. Beside her was a younger woman in a nurse's uniform holding another pink bundle. "Is it okay for me to be in here?"

Marissa settled the infant against her shoulder and set the chair in motion. "This is a community room for volunteer cuddlers of both genders to spend time with the premature babies."

"Volunteer cuddlers?"

She smiled and he felt that strange tug again—an inexplicable combination of attraction and recognition.

"There have been numerous studies done that confirm the benefits of human contact on every aspect of a preemie's development—cognitive, social and emotional," she explained. "That's the foundation of Juno's Touch."

"Juno's Touch?" he echoed again, his blood stirring in a way that reminded him how very much he'd enjoyed the goddess's touch the night before, until he firmly banished the memories from his mind.

"The Roman goddess Juno was the embodiment of the traditional female roles of wife and mother," the princess explained. "She was also the protector of the state, so it seemed appropriate—since our children are the future of not just the state but our world—to name the program after her."

It was a logical explanation, but still he wondered, "Who came up with the title?"

She seemed surprised by his question and maybe a little wary. "The board of directors approved it."

"But who proposed the name?"

"Does it matter?"

"Of course not. I was just curious," he said, trying to convince himself as much as her. Then, in an effort to change the subject, he asked, "So that's all you do here—just cuddle the babies?"

She smiled and he realized that he had underestimated the

princess again. Her demeanor might be reserved and her style somewhat bland, but she truly was a beautiful woman. And her beauty had nothing to do with her aristocratic bone structure or flawless ivory skin. Instead, it was revealed through the natural grace of her every movement, the easy curve of her temptingly shaped lips, the unexpected glint of amusement in the depths of her golden eyes. It was a beauty that came from deep within, from the honesty and integrity and compassion that were as much a part of her as the royal blood running through her veins.

"I know it doesn't seem like much," she acknowledged. "But it's a simple program that renders enormous benefits."

"But why do you need volunteers? Why don't the mothers cuddle their own babies?"

"A lot of them do," she told him. "Some of them spend twelve to eighteen hours a day at the hospital with their children. But that's not an option for everyone.

"There are so many causes of premature birth, and often the new mothers need to focus on healing themselves before they can take care of their babies. Or their babies might be in the hospital for weeks or months and they have other children at home who need their attention. For those mothers, the existence of this program gives them a much-needed break while still giving their babies much-needed attention."

"You really enjoy being part of it, don't you?"

Her smile was a little wistful this time. "There's nothing in the world like cuddling a baby. Maybe it's not rocket science, but this little guy needs me more than he needs an aerospace engineer, at least at this point in his life."

"It's obvious that you've found your calling," he said. "So why aren't you married with a dozen kids of your own already?"

"If I was, I'd hardly have any free time to spend here," she responded lightly.

"Which doesn't answer my question."

She lifted one shoulder—careful not to jostle the sleeping baby. "As old-fashioned as it may seem, I was hoping to fall in love and get married before I started having babies."

"I wouldn't say that it was old-fashioned so much as naive, especially for a woman in your position."

Her eyes flashed with fire. "You mean that a twenty-eight-year-old spinster should have given up such romantic dreams?"

He held up his hands in a gesture of surrender. "I wasn't referring to either your age or marital status but your royal title."

And as quickly as her ire had risen, it faded again. But the brief flare of temper was further proof that the princess wasn't nearly as unassuming and obedient as her mother wanted to believe.

"In that case, I apologize for jumping to conclusions."

"I apologize for being ambiguous."

She smiled again, her forgiveness coming easily in the wake of her frustration. "It wasn't your fault. I'm probably a little overly sensitive about the subject."

"If it helps, I'm no more thrilled than you are about the prospect of getting married for all the wrong reasons," he confided.

"At least you get to choose who you will marry," she said.

He frowned at that. "Are you saying that you don't?"

"Tesorian law provides for the parents of a princess to enter into a contract for marriage on her behalf, so my mother has the right to choose my husband."

"But she wouldn't force you to marry someone if you were truly opposed."

Even as he spoke the words that he hoped—for her sake—were true, he realized his error. During his brief acquaintance with the Princess Royal, he'd realized that she was a woman who liked to be in control, who would wield any power she possessed just to prove that she could.

"I hope that's an issue I won't ever have to face," she said sincerely.

"Does that mean you're not opposed to marrying me?" he asked her. When her brows lifted, he hastened to clarify. "Hypothetically, of course."

"I couldn't say for sure one way or the other, even hypothetically, because I don't know you."

Dante smiled. "Then we'll have to change that."

Marissa didn't stay at the hospital for very long after the king had gone. Usually there was nothing that soothed her soul as easily or completely as spending time with the babies, but tonight, there were thoughts and questions swirling through her mind that no amount of rocking and humming could quiet. One of those questions needed to be answered before she saw the king again the next day, so she detoured by Michael and Hannah's new home on the way to her own.

"Aunt Marissa!" Riley threw her arms around her waist and hugged her tight.

Marissa dropped a kiss on the little girl's head, then touched her lips to her brother's cheek. He looked a little unsettled, she thought, and realized that she might have come at a bad time.

"I should have called first," she apologized as Riley grabbed her hand and dragged her toward the living room.

"Of course not," he denied automatically. "We're always happy to see you."

The sentiment was confirmed by Hannah's quick smile when she saw Marissa enter the room. "This is an unexpected surprise," she said, abandoning the books she'd been sorting to give her sister-in-law a quick hug.

"We've got a surprise, too," Riley informed her.

Marissa looked from her niece, who was positively beaming, to her brother, whose expression reflected joy and terror in equal measures, to his wife, who seemed happy, if a little bit nervous, and thought she knew what that surprise was. But she didn't want to spoil Riley's fun, so she said, "What kind of surprise?"

"A really big surprise. Well, it's not really big yet. Actually, it's really, really tiny, but it's going to get really big," Riley explained. "Can you guess?"

"Hmm," Marissa said, tapping a finger against her chin. "Is it a color or a number?"

Riley giggled and shook her head, causing her pigtails to swing from side to side. "No—it's a baby! Mommy's having a baby and I'm going to be a big sister!"

Though the joy and terror in Michael's eyes had been a clear giveaway to Marissa—a man who had lost his first wife shortly after childbirth was entitled to be a little bit unnerved when his new wife announced her pregnancy—hearing the words filled Marissa's heart with a happiness that eclipsed everything else.

"That is a really big surprise," she assured Riley. Then to Hannah, "When did you find out?"

"Just now," her sister-in-law confessed, showing Marissa the stick with the plus sign in the window.

"Then this is a bad time," Marissa concluded. "You must want to celebrate—"

"We'll celebrate later," Michael said, giving his wife a meaningful look and a secret smile. "Because right now, it's Riley's bath time."

"I don't want a bath—I want to celebrate," Riley protested.

"We've got about eight months to celebrate and make plans," Hannah told the little girl. "But you've only got half an hour until your bedtime, so if you want to read the next chapter in your new book, you better get into the bath ASAP."

"Okay." Riley tugged on her father's hand. "Come on, Daddy—ASAP."

"Yes, Your Highness," Michael said, and let his daughter drag him out of the room.

Marissa smiled as she absorbed the news. She already had three beautiful nieces: Sierra, Gabriella and Cameron's now eighteen-year-old daughter, who was about to start her first year at the university in San Pedro; Jaedyn, Sierra's eleven-month-old baby sister; and Michael's five-year-old bundle of energy and inquisition known as Riley; but she was thrilled to learn that there wasn't just one but now two more babies on the way.

She was genuinely thrilled for both of her brothers and their families, and just the teensiest bit envious. "A baby," she said again.

"I know." Hannah grinned. "I've been hoping...but I was afraid to hope. And then, on my way home today, I decided just to pick up the test. Now we can stop wondering and start planning."

"You're going to be a fabulous mother—you *are* a fabulous mother."

"Thanks, but Riley makes it easy. Or maybe it was the fact that I didn't come into her life until she was almost four. This one—" she instinctively laid a hand on her still flat belly "—isn't likely to come out walking and talking, so I've got a lot to learn over the next eight months."

"Well, since you are going to have another child," Marissa began, thinking the news of her sister-in-law's pregnancy was an appropriate segue into the reason for her visit, "I was wondering if I could borrow Riley."

"Okay. As long as you return her when you're done."

Marissa had to smile at Hannah's easy response. "Aren't you even curious as to when and why?"

"When and why?" Hannah asked.

"Tomorrow for the hot-air-balloon festival at Falcon Ridge," Marissa told her. "Because I fibbed and said that I already had plans with Riley in order to avoid being alone with the man my mother wants me to marry."

"You want Riley to chaperone your date with the Duke of Bellemoro?" Hannah asked, trying to pick out the relevant details from the explanation her sister-in-law had blurted out.

"No, I want Riley to chaperone my date with the king of Ardena."

Hannah picked up the phone from the table beside her and began dialing.

Marissa frowned. "Who are you calling?"

"Gabriella. She has to hear about this."

Since Marissa figured it would be easier to tell the story to both of her sisters-in-law at the same time rather than in two separate installments, she didn't dissuade her. But she did wonder why she put the call on speakerphone.

"You need to come over," Hannah said, as soon as Gabby answered.

"Now?" The very pregnant princess sounded weary. "I just got into my pajamas—"

"So come in your pajamas," the newly pregnant princess told her. "I have big news."

"News that can't wait until tomorrow?"

"I'm pregnant and Marissa's engaged to the king of Ardena."

There was half a beat of silence before Gabby said, "I'll be there in five minutes."

The picture on the screen was fuzzy, and the more she increased the magnification of the photo, the fuzzier it got. That's what she got for working with cheap equipment. Unfortunately, since she wasn't a professional photographer, it was all she could afford. But now she worried that her efforts to pinch a few pennies might end up costing her big.

She turned her attention from the screen to the list of names beside the laptop. It was a copy of the final guest list for the masquerade ball, but even after reviewing it numerous times, she was no closer to ascertaining the identity of the mystery woman who had spent the night in Dante Romero's room at the palace.

Not that her identity really mattered, except insofar as it might add fuel to the fire of the scandal. An unmarried heiress looking for a good time? No big deal. But the devoted wife of a Tesorian cabinet member? Very big deal.

She clicked on the next photo, then the one after that. When the woman left his room in the early hours of the morning after, she carried her shoes in her left hand. Zooming in, she confirmed that the hand was bare.

With another click of the mouse, she restored the original image, looking for something—anything—that might provide a positive clue. Of course, it was hard to see anything with the damn mask covering half of the woman's face.

She clicked back through the images until she found the ones of the woman and the king locked together in a passionate embrace. She knew it was the king because she'd wheedled the location of his room out of a housekeeper, but without that knowledge, she could understand how someone might question that identification.

She rubbed the heels of her hands over eyes that were gritty from lack of sleep and too much time staring at the damn computer screen. When a familiar beep indicated an incoming text message, she snatched up her phone, her hands shaking and her heart pounding as she read her sister's message.

doctor confirmed shes doing great, should be ready 2 go home shortly, will keep u posted xoxoxo

She blew out a long breath, then replied simply:

thnx 4 update, c u soon

The message echoed in her mind and eased the ache in her heart. Tears of gratitude and relief filled her eyes, and she gave herself a moment to send up a brief but fervent prayer to express her appreciation to the big guy upstairs.

Then she turned back to the computer and the images of the king again, because she didn't owe him any thanks.

She didn't owe him anything but payback.

It was closer to twenty minutes by the time Gabriella arrived—not in her pajamas.

"I keep forgetting that I can't move as fast as I used to," she said by way of apology.

She hugged Hannah first. "Congratulations, Mommy."

Then she turned to Marissa and demanded, "Let me see the ring."

"There is no ring," she denied, shooting a look at Hannah. "I am *not* engaged. But I did have brunch with Dante Romero today."

"And she's got a date with him tomorrow," Hannah interjected.

"Well, I guess this means you were wrong about the duke," Gabby noted.

"But not wrong about my mother's plan to marry me off to a groom of her choosing."

"For once, I can't fault her choice," Hannah said.

"Ditto that," Gabby agreed.

"I feel compelled to point out that countless women around the world have reason to share your enthusiasm," Marissa said drily.

"Okay, so he hasn't exactly been…circumspect with respect to past relationships," Hannah acknowledged. "But I don't think he's been involved with anyone since he took the throne."

"Or maybe he's just learned to be discreet," Marissa suggested.

"The king does have a reputation," Gabriella acknowledged. "But it hardly rivals the one your brother built up over the years. If Cameron could change his ways, it's not impossible that Dante Romero could, too."

"Cameron changed his ways because he fell in love with you," Marissa pointed out. "Any interest the king of Ardena has in me is fueled by politics, not affection."

"It doesn't matter how something starts, only how it ends," said Hannah, who had met Prince Michael when she accepted the position as temporary nanny for his young daughter the previous summer.

"Trust me—the king is not going to propose, and I wouldn't accept his proposal if he did."

"Never say never," Gabby cautioned. "He's incredibly handsome and unbelievably charming."

"Says the woman happily married to my brother," Marissa remarked drily.

Cameron's wife only smiled. "Being married to your brother should have immunized me against other handsome and charming men, but not even I was immune to Dante Romero. And if he sets his sights on you, you won't have a chance."

"You're forgetting one important fact," Marissa reminded her sisters-in-law. "The king of Ardena will be expected to marry a virgin bride—and I no longer qualify."

Chapter Six

Security was always a concern whenever the king of Ardena attended any kind of public event, so the plan was for Dante's chauffeur to drive over to Marissa's condo first, and from there they would go together to pick up Riley. They were halfway to Riley's house when the princess's cell phone rang.

She glanced at the display. "It's my sister-in-law," she said apologetically before connecting the call.

Dante had no compunction about eavesdropping. After all, it wasn't as if he could leave the moving vehicle to give her some privacy. And while he could only hear Marissa's half of the conversation, it quickly became clear that there was a change of plans for the day. A change that, judging by the furrow between her brows and the nervous glances she sent in his direction, the princess wasn't happy about.

"Apparently Riley's running a fever," Marissa told him.

"Why do you say 'apparently'?" he asked curiously.

"Because I saw her last night and she was fine."

"Even I know kids can get sick without any notice."

"You're right," she admitted.

"But you suspect she isn't really ill," he guessed.

"I think if she was, Hannah would have sounded more worried."

"Do you think your mother somehow orchestrated the last-minute cancellation?"

"No," the princess responded without hesitation. "I can assure you that Hannah wouldn't do my mother any favors. This is entirely her own doing—her attempt to give us some time alone together."

"So I have an ally in your sister-in-law, do I?" he asked as Thomas pulled into a gravel parking lot.

"For today, anyway," Marissa grumbled. "Who can predict what she might do tomorrow?"

He couldn't help but grin in response to the obvious pique in her tone.

The chauffeur parked at the far end of the lot, away from all of the other vehicles. Several minutes passed before the door was opened and they were allowed to exit the car. Marissa knew the delay had been necessary to allow the security detail assigned to the king to survey the area and ensure there were no threats to his safety.

Her cousin, the prince regent, endured the same procedures whenever he went out. She understood that it was a way of life for a ruler and, to a lesser extent, for any royal. It was one of the reasons she preferred to keep a low profile. Unfortunately, a low profile wasn't possible in the company of the king of Ardena.

When he was satisfied that the area was secure, the chauffeur—whom Marissa suspected was likely a high-ranking member of the security team—carried a wicker basket and led the way. He guided them toward a table that had been moved some distance from the usual picnic area at the base of the nature trails—again, for security rather than privacy— while another guard followed behind.

Thomas spread a cloth over the table, then laid out the place settings and various containers of food before he bowed to the king and retraced his steps to return to the car. But Marissa knew they were not alone. So long as they remained in this public setting, there would be an invisible circle of security guards around them—and probably camera-wielding vultures in the trees.

"I was told that the best vantage point for the launch was the observation deck at the top of the trail. I was also warned that it would be impossible to secure that area because of its popularity and numerous access points, so I hope this is okay."

"This is fine," she assured him, surprised that he would even ask.

"We still have about half an hour until the launch," he noted. "Did you want to eat or walk or just relax?"

"Relaxing sounds good," she said, even as she wondered if it was possible to relax in the presence of a man who made all of her nerve endings hum.

He picked up the blanket Thomas had left on the bench and unfolded it on the grass in the center of the clearing and gestured for her to sit. She lowered herself onto the blanket, close to the edge to ensure that he had plenty of space on the other side.

He stretched out in the middle, on his back with his hands tucked behind his head and his feet crossed at the ankles.

"Is this how you like to relax?" he asked her. "By communing with nature?"

"I do enjoy being here—it's so beautiful and peaceful. In fact, I used to be a member of the Falcon Ridge Trail Walkers," she admitted. "But I stopped participating in the scheduled walks because the other members complained about the paparazzi scaring away the wildlife."

"Just one of the perks of being born royal," he noted in a dry tone.

A gust of air swept through the clearing, fluttering the leaves on the trees. Marissa tucked her knees up and wrapped her arms around them.

"Are you warm enough?" he asked her.

"I'm fine."

"You don't seem to be relaxing," he noted.

She wasn't. How could she possibly relax when he was so close? Close enough that she inhaled his tantalizing masculine scent whenever she took a breath. Close enough—

"Take off your shoes," he suggested.

"No, thank you."

"It's easier to relax when your feet are bare." He kicked off his own, then sat up to remove his socks.

She'd never thought feet were sexy. Of course, she should have realized that his would be. There didn't seem to be any part of Dante Romero that wasn't above average.

"Your turn."

"I don't…"

Her protest faltered when he reached over and picked up her foot. Suddenly her mind spun back to the night of the masquerade ball, when Jupiter removed her sandals. She remembered the way he'd unwound the lace, the slow and sensual brush of his fingers over her skin. Just the memory made her heart pound faster.

But this wasn't Jupiter, it was Dante, and he simply took hold of one shoe and tugged it off, then did the same with the other and carelessly tossed them aside.

Then he returned his attention to her now-bare feet, stroking his thumbs leisurely over the hot-pink lacquer on her toenails.

"Well, this answers one question," he murmured.

She swallowed. "What question is that?"

His gaze skimmed over her, from the ivory cowl-necked blouse to the sand-colored slacks. "Whether you disliked color."

"Neutrals are easier to coordinate," she informed him.

"But a lot less fun." He picked up one of her feet and stroked his thumb along the arch of her foot.

She didn't disagree. In fact, she didn't say anything because he was massaging her foot and she'd apparently lost the ability to form coherent thought. His thumb slid along the inside arch, circled the heel and traced the same path back again. She sighed with pleasure.

He smiled. "It feels good, doesn't it?"

"It does," she admitted. "But I'm not sure it would look good if there was a snapshot of this particular scene on the front page of tomorrow's paper."

"The area has been secured and no one knows we're even here," he told her, continuing to work his magic on her instep.

"You mean aside from the half-dozen guards patrolling the perimeter?"

"Aside from them," he agreed.

"How do you know?" she wondered.

"Because I made a point of stopping at the little café by the waterfront and asking about the beaches in San Pedro."

"Clever," she admitted.

He reached up and plucked the pins out of her hair, his movements so quick and deft that Marissa didn't even realize what he was doing until her hair was tumbling over her shoulders.

"If I'd wanted my hair down, I wouldn't have put it up," she told him, not bothering to disguise her annoyance.

"You always wear it up," he noted. "I wanted to see it down."

"And you're used to getting what you want, aren't you, Your Majesty?"

"Usually," he admitted.

She automatically scooped up her hair, but he smiled and held up the pins. With a sigh that was equal parts resignation and frustration, she released the tresses again.

"Much better," he told her and tucked the pins into his pocket. "Are you feeling more relaxed now?"

She was definitely feeling "more" something, but it wasn't relaxed. "Sure."

He shook his head, as if he knew she was lying. "It's the chemistry."

She swallowed, wondering if he was somehow able to read her thoughts. "Chemistry?"

"A physical attraction evidenced by the sparks sizzling in the air." He shifted closer, spreading his legs so that they straddled her hips while her feet were almost in his lap. "It's an elemental human response that occurs when a man and woman who are attracted to one another are in close proximity."

"You can't be attracted to me."

"It surprised me, too. Not that you're not an attractive woman," he hastened to clarify. "Just that you're not my usual type."

"Based on the extensive lineup of women you've dated, I wouldn't have guessed that you had a type."

"You might be right," he agreed. "Either way, the fact is that I like looking at you and being with you, and I can't help wondering if the attraction between us might grow into something more."

"I'm sure it's not a concern that keeps you up at night."

He was undaunted by her dismissive tone. "Of course, there's only one surefire way to answer that question."

"Maybe I don't want it answered."

"I think you do. Not consciously, perhaps," he allowed. "But subconsciously, it's preoccupying your thoughts. You're wondering when that first kiss might happen, whether you'll enjoy it, whether it will end with just one kiss or lead into something more."

If she hadn't been thinking about it before, she definitely was now. Not just thinking about it, but wanting it.

The sexy glint in his eyes warned her that he knew it.

"Instead of both of us wondering, why don't we just get it out of the way?" he suggested.

Before Marissa's frazzled brain could decipher his words, his lips were on hers.

Her first thought was that the man definitely knew how to kiss. Of course, his abundance of experience had no doubt allowed him to perfect his technique.

His mouth pressed against hers with just the right amount of pressure—enough to demonstrate that he was confident in her response but not so much that she felt his kiss was being forced upon her. He cradled her face in his hands, not to hold her immobile but only to adjust the angle of contact as he slowly deepened the kiss.

He touched the center of her upper lip with his tongue, a gentle stroke that sent waves of pulsing desire coursing through her system. Her lips parted and he slipped inside.

He continued to kiss her, continued to spin a seductive web around her, so that she was enveloped in layer after layer of sensation. Heat. Hunger. Need.

She wasn't accustomed to feeling like this, to wanting like this. But there was no denying that she did want him. She wanted him to kiss and touch her all over. She wanted to feel his lips and his hands on every part of her body. Mostly, she wanted to once again experience all those glorious sensations that had rocketed through her system when she'd made love with Jupiter.

Except that Dante wasn't Jupiter and this wasn't an anonymous encounter.

She pulled away from him and forced a smile. "Well, now that we got that out of the way, we should eat."

"I wouldn't say that we got anything out of the way," he denied. "In fact, I'd say that what we did was put the attraction between us front and center."

It was the promise in his eyes more than the words that made everything inside her quiver, but she refused to let him see it. "It was just an elemental human response to proximity," she said, turning his words back on him.

"Then I'll just have to ensure we maintain close proximity."

She ignored the heat that filled her cheeks.

"Lunch?" she prompted.

"Good idea." He grinned wickedly. "I'm starving."

Marissa couldn't help but be impressed by the selection of food. There were French breads and savory crackers, gourmet cheeses, thin slices of smoked salmon, duck foie gras with port wine and black Ardenan olives. They watched the balloons overhead as they leisurely sampled the various offerings, sipped on a crisp, chilled Chardonnay, and then nibbled on fresh fruit and dark chocolate truffles for dessert.

When they were finished, Marissa began packing up the leftovers in the basket Thomas had left. She found an unopened plastic container.

"What's this?" She didn't wait for a response but opened the lid, lifting a brow when she recognized the contents. "A peanut-butter-and-jelly sandwich?"

"I didn't know if Riley would be fond of pâtés and cheeses," he explained.

"That was very thoughtful," she said, noting that there

were also chocolate-chip cookies and a bottle of apple juice for the little girl.

"Well, I didn't actually pack it myself," he admitted. "But I'm not so self-absorbed that I wouldn't realize a five-year-old might prefer a simpler meal."

"There was a time when Riley didn't want to eat anything but chicken nuggets," Marissa admitted. "And while her eating habits are a little more expansive these days, she would definitely have gone for the peanut butter and jelly."

"You seem very close to her," he noted.

"I spent a lot of time with her when she was a baby, after Michael lost his wife," Marissa explained.

"He's remarried now, isn't he?"

"Yes, just this past spring," she confirmed. "And he and Hannah have another baby on the way, which Riley is absolutely thrilled about."

"I get the impression you're pretty thrilled, too."

She shrugged. "It's no secret that I'm a sucker for babies."

"My mother's going to love that about you."

"Be careful," she warned. "A woman could get ideas when a man talks about her meeting his parents."

"Well, it is traditional for a man to introduce his future bride to his family."

"So all those headlines about the king of Ardena searching for a queen aren't just rumor?"

"No, they're all true." He popped an olive in his mouth. "Well, all except the one about my alien bride."

She smiled at that. "Does your constitution require that a king be married?"

"It's not a requirement so much as an expectation, and the constitution provides far more latitude than do my parents."

Marissa was familiar with the weight of parental expectations. Although Elena had always demanded far more of her sons than her daughter, with both Michael and Cameron happily married now, the focus had shifted. She understood that her mother's determination to see her married to Dante Romero had nothing to do with wanting a suitable match for her daughter and everything to do with the stature she herself would gain as the king of Ardena's mother-in-law.

"But my parents are anxious for me to marry, not only because they believe our country needs a queen but because they're both eager for a grandchild."

"An heir for the next generation," she noted.

His brows lifted. "Actually, I'm not sure either of them is thinking about the future of the throne so much as their desire to have a baby around to spoil."

"What are your thoughts on that?"

"I like kids," he said easily. "And my dad was a great dad, so I'd hope I could do a decent job following in his footsteps."

"I met your father once," she told him.

"He didn't tell me that."

"He probably doesn't remember."

Dante's brows drew together. "Why would you say that?"

"Because it was more than twenty years ago."

"Really?"

"King Benedicto was in Tesoro del Mar for meetings with my uncle, and I was visiting the palace with my brothers. Of course, my brothers were running through the halls at full speed, as desperate to leave me behind as I was to keep up, and as I was racing up the stairs, I tripped and scraped the skin off of both of my knees."

Dante winced sympathetically. "That must have hurt."

She nodded. "And I screamed so that everyone would know it. Your dad was the first on the scene.

"He immediately scooped me up off the floor and carried me over to the wing chairs by the windows overlooking the rose garden. He cuddled me until my sobs subsided, then he sat me on the edge of one of the chairs and squatted down, carefully inspecting first one knee and then the next. The nanny hurried over with antiseptic cream and bandages and tried to send the king away so that she could tend to my injuries, but he insisted on cleaning and bandaging the scrapes himself. Then he took a handkerchief out of his pocket, wiped away the last of my tears, kissed my forehead and pronounced me good to go."

"That's quite a detailed memory," he remarked, sounding more than a little skeptical.

Marissa just smiled. "Every girl remembers the first time she falls in love."

"You fell in love with my father?"

"He was the first man—aside from my own father, who had passed away six months earlier—to hold me while I cried."

"That's your criteria for giving your heart?"

Her smile widened. "He was also very handsome."

"I've been told I'm the spitting image of King Benedicto when he was crowned, thirty-five years ago," he said, the devilish twinkle in those dark eyes assuring her that he was teasing.

She narrowed her gaze, as if struggling to see the resemblance. "You do have his ears," she finally acknowledged.

"And his charm?" he prompted hopefully.

"There's definite potential."

As Thomas drove back toward Marissa's condo later that afternoon, Dante found that he was genuinely reluctant for the day to end. He'd had a good time with the princess—she was easy to talk to and didn't hesitate to speak her mind on any number of topics, nor was she the least bit shy about letting him know when her ideas and opinions differed from his own.

He'd accepted the fact that he was attracted to her. What

surprised him was to realize how much he actually liked her. And that he could imagine himself spending the rest of his life with her.

Not that he was anxious to exchange vows, but he'd resigned himself to the necessity of it. And since he figured she had a right to know what his intentions were, he said, "I think we should get married."

Her brow lifted, but she replied in a similarly casual tone. "I think you're insane."

He grinned, because her response proved that his instincts about her were exactly right. He needed a wife who would stand up to him and say what was on her mind. "I realize that a marriage between us might seem impulsive—"

"Might?"

"But if you think about it," he continued as if she hadn't interrupted, "there are several valid reasons for us to marry and really no reason for us not to."

"How about the fact that I don't want to marry you?"

"Putting aside for now the fact that you acknowledged your wishes might not be a factor," he said, "why wouldn't you want to marry me?"

"Do you want a list?"

His brows rose. "Do you have one?"

"I could make one," she assured him. "And right at the top would be the fact that I don't even know you."

"I'm not suggesting we get married tomorrow."

"Well, in that case…" She paused as if reconsidering his offer, then shook her head. "The answer would still be no."

He cocked his head. "You really don't want to marry me?"

"Did you think I was being coy?"

The possibility had crossed his mind, and he realized that was his mistake. She wasn't the type of woman who played those kind of games, which was just one more thing he liked about her.

"No," he admitted. "But I do think your rejection was as impulsive as my proposal."

She didn't dispute the possibility.

"I have no desire to marry a woman against her will, but another man might not feel the same way," he cautioned.

"So you're saying that I should marry you because it's probably going to be the best offer I get?"

"No, I'm saying that you should give me—give *us*—a chance," he clarified.

"Isn't that what today was about?"

"Today was a first date. I'm asking for a second."

"Why?" she asked warily.

"Because I think your refusal to consider a relationship between us is more about resenting your mother's manipulations than any personal feelings toward me."

"I would think you would resist being manipulated as much as I do."

"I would," he agreed, "if I felt I was being manipulated."

"We both know you're not really interested in me."

"I'd say that kiss we shared in the park proves otherwise."

"You're making a big deal out of one little kiss," she warned him.

He just smiled, confident that their next kiss would prove otherwise. "I'm not asking you to run away to Ardena with me yet," he continued. "I just want a chance to get to know you."

"Because marrying a princess from Tesoro del Mar would be a strategic political move," she guessed.

"It would be foolish of me to deny that's true. However, the woman I choose as my bride—as my country's future queen—will be my wife for the rest of my life, and I have no intention of making that decision solely on the basis of political considerations."

"What other factors are there when you're responsible for the future of your country?" she challenged.

"Attraction. Affection. Intelligence. Compassion. Common interests. I don't want to stare into my coffee cup every morning because I can't carry on a conversation with the woman seated across the table from me."

"Sounds like you've given this some thought," she noted.

"Aside from international trade relations, the domestic economy, rising unemployment, health care and funding for education, I've hardly been able to think about anything else."

Her lips curved, just a little. Just enough to distract him with thoughts of how sweet those lips had tasted and how passionately she'd responded to his kiss.

"Well, that list certainly puts the matter of marriage into perspective," she said.

"Except that it is important. My parents' relationship taught me that having a true partner in life can make dealing with all of the other issues if not easier, at least manageable."

"You were lucky to have that kind of example."

"I know," he admitted. "And although I may not know you very well, the one thing I can say with absolute certainty is that you don't bore me."

"I'm so pleased to hear that, Your Majesty."

He grinned in response to her dry tone. "I imagine you'd be more pleased if I went back to Ardena and never bothered you again."

"As if spending time with the king of Ardena could ever be considered a bother."

"I'm having dinner with your cousin and his wife Tuesday night," he told her. "It will just be a small group, including the French ambassador and his spouse, and Prince Harry and his current companion. I'd be pleased if you could join us."

"I don't know how anyone could refuse such a gracious invitation."

He chuckled. "But no doubt if you did, you would."

Chapter Seven

There were three messages on her machine when Marissa got home after her outing with Dante. She predicted, even before she listened to them, that there would be one each from Elena, Gabriella and Hannah. Each one, of course, wanting to hear the details of her date with the king of Ardena.

She didn't return any of the calls because she hadn't yet decided how many of those details she was willing to share. Except that she absolutely would *not* tell her mother that he'd ever brought up the idea of marriage, because she knew that if she did, Elena would somehow manage to have the church booked before she even hung up the phone.

Except that the king of Ardena would be expected to marry in his own country so that his people could share in the celebration. The date would probably even be declared a national holiday, so that men, women and children could line the streets and wave flags. And if she was to make the list that Dante had asked her about, that would be the number-one reason why she didn't want to marry him.

I think your refusal to consider a relationship between us is more about resenting your mother's manipulations than any personal feelings toward me.

Number two: he was arrogant and smug.

Except that he was right, dammit.

Number three: he was far too insightful for her peace of mind.

She sank down on the edge of her sofa and reached for the remote. She didn't usually watch a lot of television, but she was in the mood for some mindless entertainment—or maybe desperate for any distraction that might push thoughts of Dante Romero out of her mind.

The knock at the door was a welcome reprieve. Even more welcome than her sisters-in-law was the plate of frosted brownies Gabriella carried.

"My mother baked today," she said, passing the plate to Marissa. "And since I've already gained a gazillion pounds with this baby, I thought I would bring these over to you."

"And as a heartfelt thank-you, I'll put on a pot of decaf."

While Marissa ground the beans, Hannah got out the cream and sugar and Gabby set out plates and napkins.

"Marissa?"

She looked up to see both of her friends watching her with concern.

"Sorry, I guess my mind wandered."

Gabby gestured to the plate of brownies. "I asked if you wanted one with or without nuts."

"Actually, I don't want either one right now."

"Are you feeling ill?" Hannah teased, because it wasn't like Marissa to ever turn down chocolate.

She carried the pot of coffee to the table. "Maybe I am,"

she said, looking directly at Hannah. "Maybe I picked up whatever bug it was that kept Riley home in bed today."

Michael's wife met her gaze evenly. "It was a headache that miraculously cured itself."

Gabby picked up quickly on the pointed reference to Marissa's own excuse for allegedly missing the ball.

"Riley was supposed to chaperone Marissa's date with the king," she remembered.

"Speaking of your date," Hannah said, anxious to get to the point of their visit. "How was it?"

"The balloons were spectacular," Marissa said. "It must have been a record launch, because I don't remember ever seeing so many before."

"We don't want to hear about the balloons," Gabby told her.

"What do you want to hear—details about how we did it in the back of his car?"

"Only if it's true."

Marissa had to sigh. "Only in my dreams."

"Oooh." Hannah reached for a second brownie. "Now this is getting good."

"It's not good," Marissa denied. "I'm not the kind of woman who indulges in sexual fantasies—"

"First of all," Gabby interrupted, "every woman should have fantasies. And if you've never had them before, it's probably only because you've never known anyone like Dante Romero."

"You're saying this is normal—to lust after a man I've only just met?"

"It is when that man looks like the king of Ardena," Hannah assured her.

"Wanting someone based on a purely physical attraction seems rather…shallow," she worried.

"Shallow, absolutely. Abnormal, no," Gabriella assured

her. "I fell in lust with your brother the first time I laid eyes on him."

"Me, too," Hannah said, then hastened to clarify, "but with your other brother."

"Seriously in lust?" Marissa pressed. "As in heart pounding and knees quivering?"

"And your blood pulsing in your veins so that you feel hot and tingly all over," Gabby added.

"And your body aching so desperately that you think you'll die if he doesn't touch you," Hannah finished.

"That about sums it up," Marissa agreed.

Gabby nodded. "Perfectly normal."

Even if it was normal, it was completely outside of Marissa's realm of experience. Because aside from the single night she'd spent with Jupiter, she had no experience.

"So what am I supposed to do about it?" she wanted to know.

"What do you want to do?" Hannah asked.

"I want to get naked with him." She pressed her hands to her cheeks. "And I can't believe I just said that out loud."

"Your secret is safe with us," Gabby promised her.

"I've never wanted to get naked with anyone before. Well, except for the night of the ball, and then it was for a specific purpose and not just because I'd met some guy who turned me inside out with lust." She worried her bottom lip. "Do you think losing my virginity turned me into a slut?"

Gabby snorted. "Not likely."

"How do you know?"

"Because I know *you*. And if you were easy, you *would* have had sex with him in the back of his car."

"Except that he doesn't want to have sex with me—he wants to marry me. Or he thinks he does."

"There are worse things than marrying a man who makes your blood hum," Hannah noted. "Not that sexual attraction alone is a good foundation for a lasting relationship, but it's a definite plus."

"Attraction aside for a minute," Gabriella said. "What else do you know about the guy?"

"He takes his responsibilities seriously. He wants to do what's best for his people, even when that means making unpopular decisions. When he talks about his family, you can hear the genuine affection in his voice. And when he asks a question, he actually listens to the answer. He's attentive and charming—maybe too charming. And he's considerate. When he thought that Riley was going to be with us today—" she slanted another look at Hannah "—he had a special lunch prepared for her."

"It sounds like you actually like him," Gabby noted, surprise in her voice.

She sighed. "I think I do."

"Why is that a problem?" Hannah wanted to know.

"Because it's not something I can put on my list of reasons not to marry him."

Marissa had been taught, at a very early age, that a princess had to have standards. So she never went out in public unless her outfit was coordinated, a minimum amount of makeup was applied and her hair was neatly groomed. But she didn't believe in spending an inordinate amount of time on her appearance, and she'd never been the type to primp in an effort to impress a man.

But as she dressed for dinner at the palace Monday night, she was conscious of the king's comment about the lack of color in her wardrobe. Though he hadn't said anything that wasn't true, the criticism had still stung. So she took extra care with her makeup, adding a touch of smoky shadow to her eyelids, an extra coat of mascara and a slick of gloss just a little bit darker than her usual shade.

Assessing the results in the mirror, she decided that the differences were noticeable but not drastic. The biggest change, and thankfully not one that anyone else could see, was the unexpected tangle of knots in her stomach. A tangle of knots that had nothing to do with going to dinner at the palace and everything to do with the identity of her date.

She'd offered to drive herself so that she could leave whenever she was ready, but he insisted on sending a car, refusing to listen to her argument that it was impractical for his chauffeur to drive from the palace to pick her up and take her back to the palace. Not that she minded having someone else do the driving for her—it was simply a luxury to which she wasn't accustomed.

A quick glance at the clock revealed that she had three minutes before Thomas was expected to arrive. She used those minutes to spray a quick spritz of perfume, double-check the contents of her jeweled clutch (ID, emergency cash, cell phone, lip gloss) and slip her feet into her shoes.

As if on cue, a knock sounded at the door.

"You're punctual," she said, opening the door.

The smile she had ready for Thomas faltered when she saw the king standing in the foyer, wearing formal evening dress—a black dinner jacket and trousers with a white collared shirt and black bow tie—and looking even more handsome than any man had a right to look.

"So are you," he noted, appreciation glinting in his eyes as they skimmed over her.

"Your Majesty." She curtsied automatically. "I wasn't expecting you."

"Is it not customary for a man to pick up his date?"

"Customary but not necessary," she said.

"I decided that I wanted to walk into the dining room with you, so that everyone knows we're together."

"What do you mean 'everyone'?"

"Well, Harry, specifically."

"Sounds like there's a story there," she mused.

"Not a very interesting one," he assured her.

"Perhaps I'll have to ask the prince for his interpretation of events."

"Okay, if you must know, I invited a lady friend to attend a gala event in London last year. As we were coming from different directions, we agreed to meet at the venue. Unfortunately, I got tied up on a conference call and arrived just as she was leaving."

"With Prince Harry," she guessed.

He acknowledged this with a short nod.

"Did her defection break your heart or bruise your ego?"

"Neither, really," he admitted. "But it was a lesson learned."

"Do you really think I'm the type of woman who would go home with someone other than the man who invited her?"

"I didn't think you were the type of woman who would go home even *with* the man who invited her, at least not on a second date," he teased. "But now you've given me hope for the evening."

Marissa felt her cheeks flush. *If only he knew...*

Dante had invited Marissa to be his date for dinner because her presence would round out the table and because he wanted to spend time with her. His reasons were no more complicated than that. But as he watched her across the table, chatting comfortably with the French ambassador—in French, of course—and flirting casually with Prince Harry, he realized that he was seeing yet another side of the multi-faceted princess.

For the most part, she chose to downplay her royal status. She had come into a substantial trust fund on her twenty-fifth birthday, but she maintained a modest lifestyle. Her condo was in a secure building in an exclusive neighborhood, but she lived alone, without any staff to attend to her. She drove her own car—a late-model Japanese compact—and even shopped for her own groceries.

And yet, as much as she might try to pretend she wasn't royal, when the occasion warranted, she slipped into the princess role as gracefully and effortlessly as any other woman might slip into a cloak. He found it fascinating to watch the transition, and realized her adaptability was just one more reason that she would fit easily into his world.

The only question, as far as he could tell, was whether or not she wanted to. Not that he was going to make the mistake of bringing up that topic of conversation again. At least not just yet.

For now, he was simply going to enjoy being with her.

After dessert and coffee in the parlor, when the guests started to take their leave, Dante turned to Marissa.

"Shall we take a walk in the garden?"

She had seemed comfortable and relaxed through most of the evening, chatting easily with the other guests, but the prospect of leaving the group to be alone with him gave her pause.

"It's late," she said. "I really should be getting home."

"Not so late," he assured her.

"I have an early meeting at the school board tomorrow."

"A short walk," he cajoled. "It's too beautiful a night to waste."

"All right." She relented and followed him out to the terrace.

She paused at the top of the wide stone steps, and he offered his arm to help her navigate the descent. She smiled as she tucked her hand into the crook of his elbow.

"A king and a gentleman," she noted.

"When the occasion warrants," he told her.

But the feelings that stirred in his belly weren't very gentlemanly when he caught a glimpse of the long, lean leg revealed by the slit up the front of her dress.

The dress itself had been a pleasant surprise to Dante. It was a strapless column of pale lavender silk that lightly skimmed the length of her body. It was feminine and elegant, and she truly looked beautiful in it.

On her feet she wore silver slingbacks that showed just a hint of her hot-pink toes and matched the silver clutch she carried. Her hair was swept up in some kind of twist, and the diamonds at her ears and looped around her wrist winked in the moonlight.

"Did I tell you how beautiful you look tonight?" he asked when they'd reached the bottom of the steps and he managed to tear his gaze away from her legs. "You look good in color."

"Well, there isn't a great selection of formal wear in beige," she said, tongue-in-cheek, as they started along the flagstone path.

"And I'll bet you bought this dress because you thought the color was understated."

"It is."

"No," he denied. "It's intriguing. Just a hint of purple—and maybe a hint of the woman who's wearing it."

"You're reading a lot into the color of a dress," she mused.

"I just can't help wondering why you try so hard not to draw attention to yourself."

"Maybe because I got far too much attention growing up simply by virtue of the fact that I was Prince Cameron's younger sister. He liked to party and he liked women, and the paparazzi loved him for it. And when I entered the social scene, they automatically gravitated toward me, assuming I would generate the same kind of headlines. I lost friends and boyfriends because there's no privacy or intimacy in a crowd. So I made a point of dropping off of the radar, and the paparazzi got bored and moved on."

Sadly, he could understand what she'd been through and why she'd made the choices she'd made. "And yet," he mused, "the media always seems to know when you're at a cultural event or charitable function."

She smiled, just a little. "I have no objection to putting myself in front of the camera for a good cause, but I'm not interested in peddling some designer's fashions for the style pages."

"Smart and savvy," he mused.

She led him into a private garden with fountains and columns and the scent of roses in the air.

"The first time Rowan proposed to Lara, it was in this garden," she told him.

"The first time?"

"They had an interesting—and quite public—courtship."

"I don't remember hearing about that."

"It was a lot of years ago now," she told him. "But it was a very big deal at the time—the prince regent of Tesoro del Mar falling in love with a nanny from Ireland."

"I didn't think a royal was allowed to marry a commoner without relinquishing his position in line to the throne."

"Not then, although Rowan has since changed the law. At the time, he had to hold a referendum to ensure the public approved before he could marry her."

"What if he'd lost the referendum?"

"I think he would have given up his title before he would have given up Lara." She sighed, perhaps just a little wistfully.

"Why didn't your cousin revoke the provision that allows your mother to arrange your marriage?"

"Because it's one of those laws that has been on the books

but unused for so long that no one even thinks about it anymore."

"What if you refused to go through with a marriage your mother arranged?"

"I wouldn't," Marissa admitted.

"Because the controversy would put you right in the center of the media spotlight," he guessed.

She didn't deny it.

"That's your biggest objection to getting involved with me, isn't it?"

"It's a factor," she admitted.

He stopped in the middle of the path and turned to face her. He tipped her chin up, saw the wariness battling with desire in the golden depths of her eyes.

She thought he was going to kiss her again. She *wanted* him to kiss her again, maybe as much as he wanted to kiss her. But while he might be eager to indulge in the sweet flavor of her lips, he didn't like to be predictable.

So instead of lowering his head to kiss her, he stroked his finger along the line of her jaw...to the full curve of her lower lip...across her cheek...to trace the outer shell of her ear.

She held herself still, but didn't manage to suppress the instinctive shiver that proved to Dante she was not immune to his touch.

"I'm going back to Ardena at the end of the week," he told her.

She nodded, but he thought he caught a flicker of disappointment in her eyes—or maybe that was just wishful thinking.

"I'd like you to come with me," he told her.

"Why?"

"Because I want the citizens of Ardena to get to know you before you are introduced to them as their new queen."

For about three seconds, she was absolutely speechless.

And then she said, "If that's your idea of a proposal, it could use some work."

He grinned. "I promise you, I'll do better when I'm ready to put the ring on your finger. For now, I was only trying to reassure you that my intentions are honorable."

She frowned. "You hardly even know me. How do you know you want to marry me?"

"Because you don't want to marry me."

"Are you really that perverse?"

He chuckled at the obvious bafflement in her tone. "If you think about it, it makes perfect sense."

"Sorry, but I don't see it."

"I haven't had a serious or exclusive relationship with anyone in the past several years, so in my efforts to find a wife, I'm having to start at square one. There are a lot of women who would willingly line up to be my bride, but most of them are more interested in my title and my wealth than me. But you're already a princess and you have your own income, so I don't have to wonder about your agenda."

"Then maybe the question shouldn't be 'why would you want to marry me?' but 'why would I want to marry you?'"

"Apparently I'm quite a catch," he told her.

"That whole 'ruler of your own country' thing doesn't really impress me," she warned.

"So tell me what does."

"Well, I did notice that you made an effort to keep the ambassador's wife entertained during dinner," she admitted. "You realized that she wasn't comfortable joining in the discussion about international politics, so you engaged her in a conversation about books and movies."

"I wasn't really enjoying the discussion about politics, either," he said lightly.

She tilted her head, studying him.

"Why are you looking at me like that?"

"I'm trying to figure you out."

"I'm not that complicated."

"I wouldn't have thought so," she admitted. "My first impression was of arrogance and entitlement, which was what I expected. After all, you're royal and rich and charismatic. But during the time that I've spent with you, I've realized that you're also insightful, charming and surprisingly self-effacing."

"So you do like me?"

She smiled. "I have enjoyed your company over the past couple of days."

"But?"

"But I think you're shortchanging yourself by seeking a marriage with political benefits rather than pursuing a romantic relationship."

"I'm not opposed to romance," he told her.

"I'm sure you've been responsible for some grand romantic gestures over the years."

His gaze narrowed. "And yet you still sound skeptical."

She shrugged. "It's easy when you've got a secretary who can order favorite flowers for your companion du jour, or make all the necessary reservations for a romantic candlelit dinner in Venice or Paris or Beijing, depending on the cuisine you crave, of course."

He didn't let his gaze shift away, knew that doing so would be an admission of complicity and provide the princess with yet another round of ammunition to use against him. Instead, he only said, "I would take you not to Paris but Bretagne—there's a little café on Rue Vieille du Temple that serves the most exquisite crepes."

"Okay, I'm impressed that you remember what I ate at brunch the other day," she admitted. "But I'm still not going to pack my bags and hop on a plane."

"I bet your mother would approve of your decision to take a trip with me," he said.

She narrowed her gaze on him. "Except that I haven't decided to take a trip with you."

He didn't know what else he could do or say to change her mind; he only knew that he had to because he'd promised his mother that he would find a way to get the princess to Ardena. Kidnapping seemed a little extreme and not likely to win him any points. Putting a bug in her mother's ear might be less criminal, but would undoubtedly win him even fewer points.

Now that he knew the origin of her distrust of the media, he understood why she would be reluctant to accompany him when he went home. Because the moment she stepped off the plane in the company of the king of Ardena, the press would be all over her.

But, as he suddenly recalled, she had no objection to putting herself in front of the camera for a good cause, and he just happened to have a good cause that needed some attention.

"Okay, I've tried bribery and blackmail," he acknowledged, "which leaves me only with begging."

"Why would you be begging?"

"Because I need your help."

She still looked wary. "My help with what?"

"With the upcoming charity auction for the pediatric wing at Mercy."

"What can I do?"

"Attend the event as my guest."

She turned away. "I don't think so."

He stepped in front of her again. "Why not?"

"Because I can't see how my attendance would be the least bit helpful."

"You underestimate your appeal, Princess."

She shook her head. "I don't think so."

"We're two years behind schedule on this project," he admitted. "But if this auction brings in the kind of money that I think it can, we could finally push forward with our plans."

"I'd be happy to make a donation—"

"I don't want your money. I just want a few hours of your time."

Her hesitation gave him hope. And while his invitation had been borne of desperation, he was pleased he'd followed the impulse, confident that her desire to remain in the background would succumb to her genuine desire to help a truly worthwhile cause.

"When is the auction?"

"October fifteenth."

She nibbled on her bottom lip. "I'm sure you know a lot of women—beautiful and famous women—whose presence would bring the media out in droves."

"I don't know anyone who advocates as passionately for the needs of children as you do."

"I'm flattered, really," she told him.

"But?" he prompted.

"But I'm also worried that my attendance might be misinterpreted," she admitted.

He'd considered the same issue—albeit with less concern—because he knew that being seen in the company of the princess could help repair some of the damage that too many years of indiscretion had done to his reputation.

"I'm surprised that you would weigh the nuisance of potential rumors against the benefits of a successful event," he mused, injecting just a hint of disappointment into his tone.

Her lips curved, just a little. "I'll give you an A for effort, Your Majesty, but I'm not that easily manipulated."

"Forget the A and give me a 'yes' in response to my invitation."

"Maybe."

"Well, that's better than a 'no,'" he acknowledged.

Chapter Eight

Marissa thought about Dante's request for a long time. She wanted to say yes because the hospital auction was exactly the sort of event she was happy to endorse. And she wanted to say no because she was worried that being with Dante could jeopardize her heart. Gabriella was right—she did like him. A lot. And the more time she spent with him, the more she liked him.

But in the end, she decided it wasn't fair to turn down his request for such decidedly personal reasons. Her only remaining concern was the advanced state of Gabriella's pregnancy.

She hated to think that she might be out of the country when her sister-in-law went into labor. Despite Gabriella's reminder that she still had more than two months until her scheduled due date, Marissa didn't give Dante her final answer about the auction until she had exacted a promise from the mother-to-be that she wouldn't have the baby until Marissa was home.

After she confirmed her plans with the king, she told Elena. Although her mother wasn't happy that her daughter was going to Ardena without a ring on her finger, she was thrilled that she was going. She was certain the trip was a prelude to a proposal, and she took Marissa aside to impress upon her the importance of being properly chaperoned whenever she was with the king to avoid even the suggestion of impropriety.

Marissa was tempted to tell her mother that it was too late to worry about her virtue, just to see how Elena might respond to that snag in her plans. But, of course, she didn't. And with as much trepidation as anticipation, Marissa began to prepare for her trip to Ardena.

In the last few days before her scheduled departure, she spent a lot of time at the hospital. She double- and triple-checked the volunteer schedule until Dr. Marotta took it away from her, promising her that they would somehow manage to take care of the babies and ensure the hospital walls didn't fall down during the few weeks that she would be gone.

Banished from the nursery, Marissa went down to the cafeteria for a muffin and a cup of coffee. She had just settled at a table when she sensed someone approaching.

"Excuse me, Your Highness."

She looked up to see a young woman standing beside her. Actually, she looked more like a teenager in her faded jeans and T-shirt with a backpack slung over one shoulder. A pretty teenager, with dark blond hair, mossy-green eyes and fingernails that had been bitten to the quick.

Marissa was aware that reporters came in all sorts of disguises, but she quickly decided that this girl was harmless enough and gestured for her to sit.

"I'm Naomi," she said.

"What can I do for you, Naomi?"

The girl shook her head. "I don't want anything from you. I just wanted to warn you."

"About what?" Marissa asked, more curious than alarmed.

"The king of Ardena."

Now her curiosity was definitely piqued. "Why do you think I need to be warned about the king of Ardena?"

"Because I heard that you're going out with him."

The girl might not be a reporter, but that didn't mean Marissa could trust her not to sell to the tabloids any information she might disclose. Experience had taught her that "a source close to the princess" was sometimes a stranger who had stood next to her in an elevator or taken her order from behind the deli counter at the supermarket.

"You shouldn't believe everything you hear," she advised.

Naomi, obviously expecting a confirmation or denial, seemed startled by the reply. But then she nodded. "You don't know me, so you have no reason to trust that what I'm telling you is true. But you need to know that the king has secrets."

"That's a rather vague allegation," Marissa said gently.

She didn't want to sound dismissive, but she didn't want to encourage the continuation of this conversation, either. Whatever the girl's grudge against Dante—and it seemed apparent that she had one—it wasn't any business of hers.

"If you don't believe me, ask him about Siobhan."

"Who is Siobhan?"

Naomi shook her head as she pushed back her chair. "It's not my story to tell."

Well, that was…bizarre, Marissa decided, as she watched the girl walk away.

And yet, it was hardly the most bizarre conversation she'd ever had with a stranger. For some reason, people seemed compelled to share the oddest information with her, as if it helped them feel that they'd made a personal connection with a member of the royal family. Marissa didn't usually mind, but there was something about the conviction in Naomi's eyes that unnerved her.

Then Dr. Marotta brought his coffee to her table and Marissa forced herself to put the girl and their strange conversation out of her mind.

The flight from Tesoro del Mar to Ardena was both short and uneventful. So short, in fact, that Marissa had little time to second-guess her decision or work herself into a panic about the media that would be waiting, in full force, to document the return of their king.

There had been no fanfare when they'd departed from the private airstrip in Tesoro del Mar, no one to see that Princess Marissa had boarded the plane with King Dante, and therefore no one to alert the royal press corps in Ardena to her presence. Marissa wasn't sure if the surprise element of her arrival would help her slip through unrecognized or if her unexpected appearance would focus more attention in her direction.

She took a deep breath as she paused by the door. Protocol dictated that she wait until the king reached the bottom of the stairs before she began her descent, but Dante surprised her—and everyone watching—by pausing on the first step to wait for her.

Now she was sure that everyone was looking at her. She forced herself to smile as she descended the portable staircase behind him. When she reached the bottom, he took her hand and gave her fingers a reassuring squeeze.

While she appreciated the gesture of support, she knew that the media would try to turn it into something more. But the king seemed unconcerned, smiling and waving as he led her across the tarmac to the waiting limo.

"That wasn't so bad, was it?" he asked when they were settled in the back and on their way to the palace.

"I'll let you know when I see the papers tomorrow."

Of course, in an era of instant communication, she didn't even have to wait that long. By the time they arrived at the palace, news of her arrival in Ardena had been tweeted around the world, captivating royal watchers in all parts of the globe with headlines ranging from Princess Bride-to-Be? and The New King's Newest Conquest? to Has the Prim Princess Tamed the Former Playboy Prince?

A statement was immediately released through the royal household's media liaison explaining that the princess was a friend of the king's who was visiting Ardena and would be in attendance at the Third Annual Dinner, Dance and Auction to benefit Mercy Medical Center. Marissa appreciated the effort, but she knew it wouldn't help. No amount of truth or fact would dissuade the media from generating the sensational headlines the public craved.

She also knew the media wouldn't be the only ones eager to scrutinize the Tesorian princess and her relationship with the king. A fact that was confirmed when she sat down to dinner with Dante's family a short while later.

On the plane, the king had given her the basic rundown on each of his family members. At twenty-nine, Jovanni—or Van, as he was called by his family and friends—was the next eldest and next in line to the throne. He was a scholar and a traveler who had studied at various and numerous institutions around the world, apparently acquiring degrees the way a tourist might pick up souvenir key chains, and now taught history and political science at the local university.

His twenty-five-year-old sister Francesca had an art history degree and a job as junior curator at the National Gallery of Art and Artifacts. And although Dante didn't mention it, a few years back, Princess Francesca had been briefly linked—at least in the press—with Marissa's cousin, Marcus Santiago.

Twenty-two-year-old Matteo had played semipro baseball in California for a couple of years, until he was caught in a compromising position with the wife of the team's owner. After that, he traveled from Las Vegas to Atlantic City, then on to Monte Carlo and Macao, somehow always managing to win greater fortunes than he lost and breaking all kinds of hearts along the way.

But it was nineteen-year-old Leticia who was considered the wild child of the Romero family. And it was she who had visited Tesoro del Mar with her father almost three years earlier, creating quite a scandal when photos of her dirty dancing with Prince Cameron were published in the local papers.

Despite being armed with this basic information, Marissa was still a little overwhelmed when she came face-to-face with the Romeros en masse. Benedicto may have given up the throne but he was still the head of the family, so he sat at the head of the table, with Arianna at the opposite end. As guest of honor, Marissa was seated to the queen's right, across from Dante. To her right was Jovanni, and next to him sat Francesa. Across from Francesca was Matteo, and beside him was Leticia.

Marissa had little experience with family meals. As children, she and her brothers had mostly been kept out of sight when their mother was entertaining, and even when she wasn't, Elena preferred to take her meals alone. But the Romeros were obviously accustomed to such gatherings, and no one seemed to worry about reaching in front of someone else or interrupting a conversation on the opposite side of the table. Marissa did her best to keep up with everything, but a couple of times throughout the meal, Dante gave her a gentle nudge with his foot under the table, followed by a pointed look in the direction of her plate to remind her to eat.

The meal was delicious, but it was the family dynamics that captivated Marissa.

Her conversations with Van confirmed that he was smart and unassuming—less expected were the quick smile and natural charm that immediately put Marissa at ease. Matt was as cocky and self-assured as she'd anticipated, a man to whom flirting was as natural as breathing. Francesca was mostly quiet and introspective, but she showed evidence of a surprising sense of humor. Leticia was the hardest to read. Despite her penchant for getting herself into sticky situations, Marissa got an impression of a sweet and surprisingly innocent young woman who was simply chafing against the limits and restrictions placed upon her by her status.

In addition to these individual impressions and the widely differing personalities of the siblings, Marissa got the sense that they were a tight-knit group. Certainly there didn't seem to be any obvious rivalries or jealousies, and especially not over the fact that Dante was now king.

They were all welcoming and gracious to Marissa, but she wasn't unaware of the looks that passed between them. And if she'd had any doubts before that she wasn't Dante's type, the curious glances and subtle inquisitions of his brothers and sisters put them firmly to rest.

After dinner, everyone went in different directions. Dante excused himself with an apology to Marissa, explaining that he had some political matters to discuss with his father; Van went to his suite to prepare a surprise quiz he planned to give to his students on Monday; and Matt headed out to meet some friends in town. Arianna went to her own quarters to attend to some correspondence; Francesca retreated to her studio to finish a painting.

"I don't have anywhere I need to be," Leticia confided to

Marissa. "But I am going to take the rest of this bottle of wine out to the terrace, if you want to join me."

"I would love to," Marissa agreed, pleased by the invitation.

She followed Dante's sister out to the back courtyard.

"Actually, I was hoping we'd have a minute to chat," Marissa said, accepting the glass of wine Leticia handed to her. "Because I wanted to thank you."

"I can't begin to imagine what for."

"For making headlines with my brother Cameron when you were in Tesoro del Mar a few years back."

"Oh." The young princess grinned. "I'd like to say we had a good time together, but the truth is, he brushed me off. He was very sweet about it, but very clear. I told my father the same thing, but he still freaked out."

Marissa sipped her wine. "Cameron freaked, too, when he saw the papers—which is, indirectly, how he and Gabriella hooked up again after sixteen years apart."

Leticia laughed. "Always glad to help. If you ever want to create a stir—or just stir up some gossip—I'm your girl."

"Just think of all that you could accomplish if you used your powers for good," Marissa teased.

"But it's more fun to be bad."

"Or at least pretend that you are."

The younger woman's gaze narrowed thoughtfully. "My big brother always did appreciate a woman who was more than just a pretty face."

"I'm flattered, I think," she said drily.

"You should be," Leticia said. "Dante has pretty high standards, and it's obvious that he really likes you."

"I can't imagine that he would have invited me to help out with the auction if he didn't."

"He actually told you that he wanted help with the auction?"

She nodded. "In fact, I have a meeting with the fundraising committee on Tuesday."

"Well, your association with the event will definitely combat some of the negative publicity that has befallen the hospital expansion."

Dante hadn't said anything to Marissa about negative publicity. He'd only commented that he believed her involvement could help raise the profile of the event and, consequently, attract more money to the cause.

Leticia topped up Marissa's glass, then her own. "Not to mention how much showing up as Dante's date will bolster his reputation after the hits he's taken."

Tingles of apprehension danced up Marissa's spine. "What kind of hits?"

Leticia winced. "You said he'd told you."

"He told me about the auction," she repeated.

"Well, then—" the princess lifted her glass "—let me wash down my foot with some pinot noir."

"What kind of hits?" Marissa asked again.

She sighed. "The press has been gunning for Dante since my father announced that he was stepping down. They've been claiming that the new king is out of touch with the needs of his people, socially unaware and fiscally irresponsible."

"That all sounds rather vague and, truthfully, not much different than the criticisms about any other form of government."

"You're right. But more specifically, there was an error made with respect to the allocation of funds in the national budget shortly after Dante took office. Somehow, money that had been earmarked for the hospital—for the purchase of equipment for the neonatal intensive-care unit—was instead diverted to the naval-defense fund."

"Why the naval-defense fund?"

"Where the money went isn't as important as the fact that

the hospital didn't get it," Leticia said. "And when a new-born's near-fatal medical condition wasn't diagnosed because Mercy didn't have the right equipment, Dante was blamed. The media alleged that he didn't care about the nation's health care or its children."

"And I've been vocal in my support of both," Marissa realized.

"I didn't mean to imply that your reputation is the only reason he's interested in you," Leticia said, sounding apologetic.

But for Marissa, the information certainly answered a lot of questions.

Dante was relieved to be home.

He was even more relieved that he'd succeeded in convincing Marissa to come back with him for the auction, which was exactly what he wanted. Or at least the first step in getting him what he wanted.

"I like your princess."

Dante couldn't help but smile in response to his father's typically blunt statement. "At this stage, I think she might object to being referred to as mine."

"Isn't she the one you're going to marry?"

"As soon as I can get her on board with that plan."

"I can't imagine that will take too long." Benedicto lowered himself into a vacant chair. "I've never known you not to get what you want."

"I'd say that the citizens of Ardena are probably more eager for a royal wedding than I am."

"You don't have to be eager but you do have to be committed," his father warned. "Marriage should be forever. If you're not sure, or if you don't think she's the right one, or if you have any doubts at all about whether she can handle the expectations and demands that will be placed upon her, then you should wait."

"I am committed," Dante assured him. He might not have been thrilled about the sudden pressure to marry, but he understood it. And he knew that he had an obligation to choose a bride who would not only make a suitable wife but an able representative of Ardena, and he was convinced that Marissa Leandres was the most appropriate choice.

Having been born a princess, she was accustomed to the intrusiveness of the media. Yet despite having lived much of her life under public scrutiny, she'd managed a mostly quiet existence without any scandals in her past or obvious skeletons in her closet. Not just a quiet but chaste existence, if her mother was to be believed. As he'd told Elena, he didn't expect a virgin bride, but he definitely didn't want an ex-boyfriend posting naked pictures of her on the internet after their engagement was announced.

Marissa was beautiful and if she'd chosen to play up her looks and dress the part, she could have coasted through life on the power of her celebrity. But she was smarter than that. Not just intelligent and well educated, but possessing a sharp mind that probed and challenged. She had ideas and opinions that she expressed articulately, and he genuinely enjoyed just talking with her.

She was kind and compassionate and was respected around the world for her charitable works. A lot of high-profile people had specific causes they endorsed or programs they funded. Marissa didn't lend her name to events for the publicity or write checks for the tax deduction. She was truly committed to bettering the lives of women and children around the globe, with a specific push toward doing so through access to better health care and education.

"What are you committed to?" his father asked now. "The concept of marriage in general or the princess in particular?"

"Both."

"Good, because you have to remember that the woman you choose as your queen will also be your wife. There will be times when it's just the two of you behind closed doors, and it's important that you can look forward to those times."

"We had the talk about the birds and the bees a long time ago," Dante reminded his dad.

"Unfortunately, we didn't also talk about good judgment. If we had, when I'd stepped down, the people wouldn't have been so concerned about a playboy running the palace."

It was only years of experience and training that ensured he didn't flinch beneath his father's steely gaze.

"But youthful indiscretions can be forgiven," Benedicto continued, "maybe even forgotten. And your behavior since taking the throne has been circumspect."

Dante felt no pride in response to his father's words. How could he when the image of the red-haired, green-eyed goddess—naked on his bed, save for the mask that concealed her face—nudged at the back of his mind? However, he could, and did, feel relief that at least he had shown *some* discretion that night. No one, not even Juno, knew that Jupiter was really the king of Ardena.

But as much as he'd enjoyed the hours he'd spent making love with Juno, he'd had an unexpected revelation when he'd woken up alone. He was tired of one-night stands. He wanted a partner. Someone not just to share his bed but to share his life.

And then he'd met Marissa, and he'd felt a surprising sense of rightness, as if everything was falling into place. Almost as if it was…destiny.

"You've had to make a lot of adjustments since February," Benedicto continued. "And you've done so without complaint."

"As much as the whole firstborn thing wasn't really my

choice, none of this is—aside from the timing—unexpected. Both you and Mom spent a lot of years not just prepping me to take the throne, but providing an example of what it takes to make a marriage succeed."

"I hope we have, because finding a comfortable balance between your duties and your desires is important in life." Benedicto smiled. "We didn't have five kids together out of a sense of obligation, you know."

"Please." Dante held up a hand. "There are certain details a son doesn't need to know about his parents' marriage."

"Fair enough," his father said. "But you should think about those details before embarking on your own."

Oh, he'd thought about those…details. And even though he'd kissed Marissa only once, that single kiss had been enough to hint at the passion within her, a passion he was eager to explore.

One step at a time, he reminded himself.

Marissa never slept easily in an unfamiliar bed, so before she returned to her room, she decided to find something to read. Upon their arrival, Dante had given her a quick tour of the palace, and she was fairly confident that she could navigate the route to the library and back to her suite.

She only took one wrong turn on the way and was happily perusing the shelves when Dante's father entered the room.

She curtsied. "Good evening again, Your Majesty."

He seemed startled to see her, as if they hadn't shared a meal at the same table a few hours earlier. And when he did address her, he said, "It's good to see you again, Elena."

Marissa was taken aback, not just to hear him speak her mother's name but by the warmth in his tone. "I'm not Elena, Your Majesty. I'm her daughter, Marissa."

He frowned, as if what she was saying didn't make any sense to him. Then the bewilderment in his eyes cleared and he smiled at her. "Forgive my confusion," he said. "I didn't realize before how very much you look like her."

"Do you know my mother?"

"I did, a very long time ago."

Which surprised Marissa, but not nearly as much as his next statement.

"In fact, we were supposed to be married."

She frowned, thinking it likely that he had the Princess Royal confused with someone. Because if Dante's father had been engaged to Marissa's mother, she was sure that detail would have come up at least once during the numerous conversations in which Elena had pushed her daughter to consider marriage to Benedicto's son.

"I'd only met her a few times," the king's father continued, "but every time, her beauty quite simply took my breath away. She thought I was quite handsome, too. At least she said that she did.

"But she was stubborn and headstrong, and regardless of her feelings for me, she refused to be forced into an arranged marriage. So while my father and her father were discussing the details of our betrothal, she ran off and married another man."

"Gaetan Leandres," Marissa murmured, familiar with at least that part of the story. "My father."

His eyes clouded again. "That might be right. It was a long time ago."

"At least forty years," she guessed, since her brother Michael was almost that age.

He nodded.

Marissa had thought she was familiar with the story of her parents' whirlwind romance, but in the version she knew, there had never been any mention of Benedicto Romero. If what Dante's father was telling her now was true, and she had no reason to suspect that it wasn't, then there was obviously a lot more to the tale than she'd ever suspected.

And she couldn't help but wonder if that "more" was somehow motivating Elena's efforts to push her daughter and the present king of Ardena together.

Chapter Nine

On Wednesday, Marissa was invited to take tea with Dante's mother in her sitting room.

After the petits fours were set out and tea had been poured, Arianna said, "I understand you don't often travel outside of Tesoro del Mar, so I wanted to express how pleased we all are that you've chosen to visit Ardena."

"His Majesty was very persuasive when he issued the invitation," Marissa told her.

The queen mother smiled. "My son inherited more than his fair share of his father's charm. As a result, it is a rare occasion when he doesn't get his own way."

"I'm sure it is."

"But I didn't invite you here to talk about Dante. I invited you here so that we could get to know one another." Arianna sipped her tea. "Considering your royal status, there's limited information readily available about you aside from your charitable endeavors."

"Have you been looking for information?"

The queen selected a pretty pink cake from a platter. "You can't blame a mother for being curious about the woman who has snagged her son's attention."

"No," Marissa agreed. "But if you're trying to determine if I'm good enough for your son, why don't we just agree that I'm not?"

Arianna seemed to puzzle over this as she sipped her tea. "Are you saying that you don't want to marry Dante?"

His mother sounded so incredulous, Marissa had to smile.

"I think he's a good man, and I've enjoyed spending time with him, but I have no interest in being his queen."

"So your only reason for coming to Ardena was to *not* have a relationship with my son?" the queen asked skeptically.

"Well, that wasn't my only reason," Marissa conceded. "I also came because Dante suggested that my attendance could help promote the auction for Mercy Medical Center."

"I'm sure it will," Arianna agreed. "But I didn't realize that was the enticement he used to bring you here."

Now it was Marissa's turn to be puzzled by her choice of words. "Are you suggesting that he had another reason?"

"Well, according to all of the newspapers, the king is courting his queen."

"The newspapers are wrong."

"Are you sure?"

"Yes, I'm sure. Dante knows I don't want to marry him."

"You've told him this?" his mother asked, amusement evident in her tone.

"Yes."

Arianna smiled. "That could be precisely why he's chosen you."

"He hasn't chosen me," Marissa said, though she was aware that the protest sounded weak.

"Perhaps not," the queen allowed. "But if he has, remember that it's rare for Dante not to get what he wants."

The queen's warning echoed in the back of Marissa's mind for the next few days. She was certain that a single conversation with Dante would answer all of her questions. Unfortunately, the king remained elusive.

After more than a week away, she could understand that he had a lot of work to catch up on. She could hardly blame him for being tied up with appointments and conferences or away from the palace for various state functions.

And she managed to keep herself busy, too. She had meetings with the fundraising committee to review and revise all manner of details for the upcoming auction. She walked in the garden and swam in the pool, and she spent a lot of time at her computer, emailing her friends and family back in Tesoro del Mar. Hannah was ecstatic in the early stages of her pregnancy; Gabriella was cranky in the last trimester of hers. And Dr. Marotta insisted that everything was running so smoothly at the hospital, no one even noticed that she was gone.

She was pouting over that one when she ventured outside to enjoy the sun on Monday afternoon and found her attention caught by some trees in the distance. As much time as she'd spent wandering the grounds, she'd never noticed them before and she couldn't resist exploring.

She tipped her head back and jolted when she saw movement out of the corner of her eye. With a self-conscious laugh, she pressed her hand to her furiously beating heart. "You scared me, Your Majesty."

"My apologies," Benedicto said. "I couldn't resist the lure of a beautiful woman in my olive grove."

"I should be the one to apologize if I've wandered where

I shouldn't have. I didn't expect to find an orchard on the grounds, and my curiosity was piqued."

"Guests are free to wander wherever they wish," Benedicto assured her. "And it has been a long time since anyone has shown an interest in my trees."

"They're beautiful," she said truthfully, letting her fingers trace a deep ridge in the gnarled trunk of the tree closest to her. "So unique and full of character."

"There's a lot of history in those twisted branches," the former king agreed. "And a lot of generations have harvested their bounty."

She noted the clusters of green fruit. "When will you pick these?"

"Actually, we don't pick them. We shake the branches," he told her. "And we usually start around the end of November, finishing in late January or early February. You're welcome to help, if you're interested. We can always use an extra pair of hands."

"I am interested," she said. But she wondered if she would still be in the country then or if, having satisfied her obligations in Ardena, she would have gone back to Tesoro del Mar.

...it's rare for Dante not to get what he wants.

But what did he want? Did he want her help with the auction or did he want something more?

Arianna's words teased Marissa's mind with possibilities. To marry the king of Ardena would mean many things. For Marissa, the biggest negative would be the complete lack of privacy. As queen, everything she said and did would be scrutinized and criticized, analyzed and interpreted. But she wondered now if there might not be enough positives to more than balance the scales. And one undeniable positive was the attraction she'd felt for the king almost from the start, an attraction that continued to grow.

"What are you interested in?"

The tantalizingly familiar voice skimmed over her like a caress, making her think of all kinds of answers to the question that had absolutely nothing to do with olive trees.

"The princess was asking about the harvest," Benedicto explained to his son.

"And mother was asking where her husband had run away to," Dante said.

Though his tone was light, Marissa heard the undercurrent of worry.

"She should have guessed I'd run away with a pretty lady," he said and winked at Marissa.

"Obviously your son comes by his charm honestly enough," she noted.

Benedicto grinned. "But be careful—he's as stubborn as he is charming," he warned. "He needs a woman with a strong backbone, someone who will not only stand up to him, but stand behind him."

"Dad—"

"I'm only trying to help your cause," Benedicto explained.

"It would be a bigger help to give us some time alone," Dante said pointedly.

"Okay," his father relented, squeezing Marissa's hand before he released it. "But don't try any hanky-panky. This one isn't just a princess. She's a real lady."

"I know."

Marissa watched Benedicto make his way back toward the palace. When Arianna met him in the courtyard, something her husband said caused her to throw her head back and laugh. Then Benedicto caught her around the waist and drew her into his arms for a kiss that made Marissa sigh.

"Your father is a wonderful man," she said to Dante now.

"He obviously thinks just as highly of you," he noted.

"I didn't realize we'd wandered out of sight. I'm sorry you were worried."

"Why would I be worried?"

"Maybe because his memory has started slipping a little," she suggested.

"Why would you say that?" he challenged.

"Am I wrong?"

Dante glanced away, back toward the house, but not before she saw the flash of pain in his eyes. "No," he admitted.

She waited for him to continue. After his father and mother went inside, he did so.

"The official diagnosis is vascular cognitive impairment," he explained. "Likely precipitated by a series of minor and undiagnosed strokes he suffered over the past two years."

She touched a hand to his arm. "I'm sorry."

"There are moments of obvious confusion, and my mother doesn't like him to wander off on his own. But his good days outnumber the bad, so we've managed to keep his condition under wraps."

"I'm not going to tell anyone," she assured him.

"I know." He caught her hand as she started to draw it away and linked their fingers together. "Thank you."

"For what?"

"For being so warm and generous, kind and compassionate, smart and strong."

She lifted a brow. "That's a pretty thorough character assessment considering you met me hardly more than a week ago."

"In that brief amount of time, I've had the opportunity to observe you in various situations," he told her. "I've witnessed your interactions with your mother—who is an undeniably strong and unyielding woman. But you don't let her push you around. You decide when to stand firm and when to give way. And I've seen you as a volunteer at the hospital, and I've watched your eyes go soft when you hold one of those tiny babies in your arms."

"You're very observant, Your Majesty."

"You're a fascinating woman, Your Highness. But aside from all of that," he continued, "I know my dad likes you. And while his mind might drift to the past occasionally, he's always been a great judge of character."

"Well, he did warn me about *you*," she said lightly.

He tugged her toward him. "You don't look very worried."

"Why would I be? You assured me your intentions are honorable."

"But 'honorable' is not synonymous with 'innocent,'" he cautioned as he reached up to tuck a loose strand of hair behind her ear, his fingertip brushing the sensitive shell as he did so.

She shivered in response to the light caress. He smiled.

"That's something else I've observed—the way your pulse races when I touch you."

She swallowed, as disconcerted by the accuracy of his insight as she was by his nearness.

"Considering your legendary exploits, I would expect you to be accustomed to the effect you have on women."

"Right now I'm only interested in the effect I have on *you*," he said, stroking a finger down the curve of her cheek.

She pushed his hand away. "Well, I'm not interested in your meaningless flirtations."

"Why do you refuse to believe that I'm attracted to you?"

It wasn't that she *refused* to believe it so much as she *couldn't* believe it. She knew she wasn't his type. She wasn't as beautiful or sexy or sophisticated as the women he usually dated, which was why she'd assumed his interest was predicated upon her title and nationality, and his belief—albeit mistaken—that she was an innocent.

"Why are you so intent on denying what's between us?"

His hands stroked up her arms, his fingertips following the ridge of her collarbone, then dipping to trace the deep V of her jacket. Heat swept through her body, making her heart pound and her body yearn, making her nipples ache for the touch of his hands. A soft sigh escaped through parted lips.

"We would be good together, Marissa. I have no doubts at all about that."

"I'm not going to fall into your bed," she told him.

"I'd be happy to carry you."

She shook her head. "I'm not the type of woman to be swept away by promises or passion."

"I don't think you know what type of woman you really are," he countered.

"But I'll bet you could show me," she said drily.

"I'd prefer for us to figure it out together." His voice was as tantalizing as his hands. "I want to watch your face when I touch you, to watch the hesitation in your eyes change to awareness and desire. I want to hear your breath catch and feel your muscles quiver. I want to kiss you, long and slow and deep."

He was seducing her with nothing more than his words, without even touching her. And if her body had felt hot and tingly before, that was nothing compared to what she was feeling now.

She had to moisten her lips before she could speak, but when she managed to respond, she was pleased to note that her voice was level, giving no hint of the desire churning in her veins. "You want a lot of things," she noted. "And if you got them, I'm sure you'd be disappointed."

"I'm sure I wouldn't be," he said. "And neither would you."

Though her experience was extremely limited, the intensity of her physical response to him warned that it wasn't an idle promise. And she knew that if he touched her again right now, she would melt into a puddle at his feet.

But he didn't.

Because Dante was afraid that if he touched her now, he

wouldn't be able to stop. And as much as he wanted her—and believed she wanted him, too—he could tell she wasn't ready to take their relationship to the next step.

So instead he only said, "Take a walk with me."

"Is that a personal request or a royal command?"

He grinned at the pique in her tone. "Whatever will get you to say yes."

He led her to the stone gazebo at the top of the hill. From there, they could see the ocean. He breathed deeply, inhaling the familiar tang of salty air that he always missed when he was away from home. But beneath the scent of the ocean, he caught a hint of Marissa's perfume, and he noticed that the breeze had caught a few more strands of her hair and tugged them free of the loose knot at the back of her head.

He gestured for her to sit, and she lowered herself onto the edge of a bench, crossing her feet at the ankles and folding her hands in her lap. Her pale yellow skirt and boxy jacket were unappealing, but there was an inexplicable something about Marissa that drew him. And he suspected that if he ever got her out of those boring clothes, he would find the Tesorian princess wasn't nearly as dull as she wanted everyone to believe, that the carefully cultivated image was nothing more than a facade, and that beneath the cool and prim shell beat a warm and passionate heart.

He sat beside her and picked up the thread of their earlier conversation. "There is a powerful chemistry between us, Your Highness. An undeniable attraction that I believe could provide a solid foundation for marriage."

"I thought you'd given up on the idea of marrying me."

"A king doesn't surrender at the first sign of opposition," he told her.

"I thought you were searching for a bride, not outlining a military campaign."

"Apparently both require careful and strategic planning in order to overcome the enemy's opposition."

Her lips curved, just a little. "Am I the enemy?"

"No," he denied. "But you need to understand that I'm not the enemy, either. I didn't write the law that gives your mother the authority to choose your husband, Marissa."

"I'm aware of that."

"And I don't blame you for feeling trapped."

Which was exactly how Marissa felt.

Trapped between the proverbial rock and hard place.

But since her mind was churning out idioms, wasn't it better to be trapped with the devil she knew? Maybe she didn't know Dante Romero very well, but she at least had an idea of what he wanted from her. If she didn't marry the king of Ardena, there was still the possibility—more likely the inevitability—that Elena would simply choose a different husband for her daughter. Maybe even the Duke of Bellemoro.

Of course, that possibility was what had driven Marisa to take such drastic action the night of the ball. At the time, she'd been confident that she was doing the right thing. In retrospect, she had to accept that giving her virginity to a stranger rather than having it taken by the duke hadn't been such a brilliant scheme since it meant she was no longer suitable to marry the one suitor she might not have objected to marrying.

But the truth was that even if she decided to marry Dante—disregarding for a moment the fact that she was no longer "pure of virtue" and therefore probably unsuitable to be the king's bride—it wouldn't really be her choice. If it was up to Marissa, she wouldn't be choosing to get married at this point in her life. She would wait until she'd fallen in love—and until the man she loved had fallen in love with her, too. Unfortunately, since the Princess Royal had decided to seek a husband for her daughter, Marissa's only choice was whether to accept her mother's decision willingly or not.

"I'm not expecting an answer right now," he told her. "I just want you to consider the possibilities. And while I'm not unaware of what you would be giving up if you were to leave Tesoro del Mar to make a life with me here, I'm confident that the trade-offs would make it worth your while."

"Such as?"

"No longer being subjected to your mother's arbitrary exercise of power."

On the surface, that sounded tempting, but she said, "Instead, I would be subjected to yours."

He shook his head. "Equal partners, Marissa. That's what I'm offering you. As my wife, you would be queen, and as the queen of Ardena you would have the opportunity and freedom to pursue your own interests. You could even continue the work you were doing at PACH in the soon-to-be-expanded pediatric wing at Mercy."

He had to know that she would be tempted by this offer. The work she'd done at the hospital in Port Augustine had been incredibly fulfilling and rewarding.

"And, at the end of the day," he continued, "when you'd finished taking care of everyone else's babies, you could come home to your own."

Her eyes lifted to his. "When you embark on a military campaign, you take the big guns, don't you?"

"The key to a successful negotiation is to know what the other party wants," he told her.

"What do *you* want?"

"I told you—a queen for Ardena, a wife to share my life, a mother for my children." He smiled as his gaze skimmed over her. "And the pleasure of taking the woman who is my wife and the mother of my children to bed every night."

She was undeniably tempted by his offer. And tempted by

the tantalizing thought of making love with him. She couldn't help but wonder what kind of lover he would be, if he could make her feel the way she'd felt when she was with Jupiter—

She banished the thought to the back of her mind. She couldn't think about him now, she wouldn't let herself consider that the most incredible night of her life might have been the biggest mistake she'd ever made.

"That's a lot to consider."

He shifted closer to her, so that his thigh pressed against hers. "Or you could trust what's in your heart and take a leap of faith."

"I trust my heart." She rose to her feet, needing to put some distance between them. "I don't trust *your* motives."

He followed her to the other side of the gazebo. "I've been completely honest about what I want."

She studied him for a minute. "Okay, but I want you to be honest about something else."

"Anything," he said automatically.

"Why did money intended for the hospital end up in the defense fund?"

He wasn't so quick to respond to that question. And when he finally did, his answer didn't make a lot of sense to Marissa.

"Because in 1982 there was a very real threat of invasion by a Greek drug cartel that wanted control of the underwater caves on the northern shores of the island."

"You would have been a child in 1982."

He just nodded.

"It wasn't your signature on the budget," she realized. "It was your father's."

He didn't confirm or deny it. He only said, "My father had already stepped down."

But Marissa wasn't fooled, and she found herself wondering what kind of man would willingly subject himself to the criticism and ridicule of his people in order to protect and preserve the reputation of his father. The answer was suddenly as clear as it was simple: a man whose love for his family was as steadfast as his loyalty to them. And she suspected that any woman lucky enough to win Dante's heart would experience the same unwavering affection and devotion.

She just didn't know if that woman could ever be her.

Chapter Ten

Marissa didn't believe that the way to a man's heart was through his stomach, but she did believe that the way to a benefactor's wallet was. In her experience, the rich were always more generous after they'd been well fed, and one of the first things she'd done when she met with the catering company in charge of the meal for the Dinner, Dance and Auction was to reconfigure the menu. If this event was to garner special attention, she argued, it needed to offer something a little more special than the typical rubber-chicken plate.

The caterers grumbled about clients wanting changes made at the eleventh hour, and insisted that her "special" menu would require "special" payment. Marissa slapped down a quote from a competitor, which outlined exactly what she wanted for the meal at a cost commensurate with what the committee had agreed to pay for the original.

But she understood that successful negotiations required

give-and-take on both sides, and while she refused to pay anything more than the contract price, she did offer to include the revised menu in the auction program, with the catering company's logo and contact information. The benefit was obvious: impress the guests with the meal, and the referral business from the high-end clientele was potentially unlimited.

So the guests who attended the event in the Grand Ballroom of the Castalia Hotel in downtown Saint Georgios were presented with baskets of artisan breads instead of dinner rolls, served tomato and bocconcini salad rather than mixed greens, and offered their choice of succulent Chateaubriand with roasted red potatoes and glazed baby carrots or grilled sea bass with wild rice and peppers and mushrooms.

Throughout the meal, diners were encouraged to browse the auction tables and make an offer on favorite items, and Marissa was pleased to note that the bidding had become quite competitive even before dessert—a delectable walnut-date torte—was served. And by nine o'clock, she was certain that the Third Annual Dinner, Dance and Auction to benefit Mercy Medical Center was going to be an unqualified success.

If she'd been nervous about anything aside from the revenues generated by the event, it was the seating plan. She was attending the auction as the king's guest, and she knew that a lot of eyes would be focused on their table throughout the evening. Thankfully, all of Dante's family was in attendance, as well, and since Van had invited a fellow professor from the university and Francesca was accompanied by her on-again, off-again boyfriend of the past three years, their table of ten was filled with people she could trust not to spend the entire meal staring at her and Dante.

Away from the table, it was a different story, of course. But Marissa was prepared for that, and since she understood that this curiosity had probably sold a lot of tickets to the event, she tried to be gracious.

About halfway through the meal, Dr. Nikolas Stamos, chairman of the board of directors of Mercy Foundation, took the podium to welcome everyone and thank them for their generous and ongoing support of the hospital and its programs. Then he spoke briefly about the history of the facility, touched on recent advances in medical science and outlined plans for the future of Mercy. He was passionate and eloquent but, most importantly, he was concise.

He'd been a little disgruntled when Marissa nixed his suggestion of a PowerPoint presentation outlining the projected costs of the expansion. But whereas she'd strong-armed the caterer, she'd sweet-talked the chairman, gently pointing out that people who had paid to walk through the door should have an opportunity to enjoy their meal without the weight of moral obligation or social responsibility being forced upon them.

The chairman had been skeptical, but in the end, he'd deferred to her expertise. And when Dr. Stamos had taken his seat again, Marissa and Dante began to work the room.

This was Marissa's specialty. She tended to steer away from crowds, but she was good with people in more intimate situations. And she was content to circulate here, taking the time to speak with anyone who wanted a word, happily discussing what she knew about the proposed hospital expansion and politely deflecting inquiries about her relationship with the king.

Dante stayed close by and proved willing to respond to whatever subjects were directed his way. He was knowledgeable and articulate, and he had a knack for connecting with people. He was charming and sincere. When he asked a question of someone else, he actually listened to the response.

And when a question was asked of him, he considered his reply rather than reciting a stock answer.

He was the king—ruling wasn't just his responsibility, but his birthright. He didn't need the approval of anyone in this room, but she realized that he wanted to at least earn their respect. He was showing them that he was accessible, willing to listen to their concerns in order to better respond to them. And Marissa was forced to acknowledge that she'd made a mistake in assuming that the new king wasn't anything more than his reputation.

She wasn't in the habit of making premature judgments about other people. As a princess, she was often subjected to stereotyping, and she should have known better than to accept the king as a particular "type." Just as she wasn't as sweet and docile and empty-headed as many believed a princess should be, she should have recognized that Dante wasn't one-dimensional.

Of course, he'd done nothing to contradict the media's image of him. From the moment they'd met, he'd flirted with and teased her relentlessly. But now she knew that the carefree playboy image he'd so carefully cultivated was just an image—the sexy charmer was undoubtedly an aspect of his personality, but it wasn't the complete definition of the man.

By the time they'd finished their circuit of the room, the band had started to play and several couples were on the dance floor. She glanced back at the table, looking for Dante's parents, and noted that the seats they'd occupied at dinner were empty.

"You're looking for someone," Dante guessed.

"Your dad," she said. "I promised him a dance."

"My parents decided to have an early night."

"Oh," she said, genuinely disappointed.

"Of course, I'd be happy to take his place," Dante said to her.

Her brows lifted. "Haven't you already done that?"

"I meant as your dance partner," he clarified, offering his hand.

She hesitated.

"Didn't the instructors at your finishing school teach you that it's impolite to decline a gentleman's request to dance?"

"They did," she acknowledged. "I just figured there was enough talk going around about our relationship without giving the crowd more reason to speculate."

"They're speculating already," he warned. "Wondering why Princess Marissa is refusing the king's gallant invitation. Doesn't she know that he's considered quite the catch—that women around the world are vying for the opportunity to be his queen, and that half of the women in this country would give almost anything for the opportunity to be held in his arms?"

"That would be the half that haven't already been in his arms?" she guessed, even as she placed her hand in his.

"Ouch."

But he was smiling as he led her into the waltz, and while Marissa had some reservations about agreeing to this dance, she couldn't fault his style. He executed the steps smoothly, so that they moved in sync with the other couples. And as they spun around the dance floor, she couldn't hold back the images that spun through her mind.

Images of the Mythos Ball and the man she knew only as Jupiter.

Maybe it wasn't surprising that the memories would be triggered by this dance. After all, she hadn't danced with anyone else since she'd danced with Jupiter that night.

Not that Dante reminded her of Jupiter in any specific way. The king was taller than the god—or maybe it was just that the shoes she was wearing tonight didn't add a full four inches to her own height. And the king's chest wasn't as broad. Of course, he wasn't wearing a breastplate, either. But there was one real and disturbing similarity, and that was the quivering excitement that originated low in her belly and slowly spread through her body.

Lust.

She recognized it now for what it was and saw no reason to romanticize the feeling. The king was an undoubtedly handsome and charismatic man and she was hardly the first woman to have lustful feelings for him. But she was likely the first who had made any effort to resist them.

"You're an excellent dancer, Your Majesty," she noted, hoping that the effort of making conversation would distract her from the blood pulsing in her veins.

"It's easy with an excellent partner," he told her. "And a sincere pleasure with a beautiful one. Have I told you how stunning you look tonight?"

She felt her cheeks flush. Though she hadn't strayed too far from her usual color palette, the slim strapless gown of chocolate-colored silk was more eye-catching than her usual attire. And while she'd promised herself that she wasn't dressing to catch the king's eye, she was pleased that he'd noticed.

"You aren't accustomed to compliments," he noted.

"I'm not accustomed to anyone looking at me the way you do," she admitted.

"And you're smart to be wary," he admitted. "Because while a man can't help but look at what he admires, he is rarely content to simply look."

And then he shifted topics as deftly as he transitioned through the steps of the waltz. "I saw you talking to the chief of pediatric medicine earlier."

"Dr. Kalidindi was interested in learning more about the volunteer-cuddler program at PACH."

"Juno's Touch."

She was surprised that he'd remembered the name—and

she was frustrated by her own inability to forget about the one night in which she'd experienced the power and freedom of being the goddess Juno.

"He's interested in launching a similar program here, and he asked if I would be willing to help get things started."

"What was your answer?"

He sounded more curious than concerned, as if her response was of no consequence to him.

"I told him I would have to think about it. I have a life and responsibilities in Tesoro del Mar that I've already neglected for more than three weeks. Not to mention that you must be anxious to get rid of me so that your life can go back to normal."

"You have to know I don't want to get rid of you, Your Highness. In fact, I'd very much like you to stay."

"Our agreement was that I would come to Ardena to help with the auction," she reminded him.

"So let's make a new agreement."

"I'm not sure it would be wise for me to stay any longer."

"Playing it safe, Princess? Or running scared?"

Both, she acknowledged, if only to herself. Aloud she said, "The song is over, Your Majesty."

"But I'm not ready to let you go."

"People are watching."

"I don't care."

"I do." She curtsied and stepped back. "I told you when I agreed to come here that I didn't want my photo splashed across the newspapers under headlines speculating about the nature of our relationship."

He fell into step beside her as she moved away from the dance floor and back to their table. "Then let's stop the speculation."

She picked up her water glass, sipped. "How?"

"By announcing our engagement."

Her heart actually stuttered, and she realized that at some point over the past few weeks, the idea of marrying the king had become less daunting and more enticing. She wasn't entirely sure when her feelings toward him had changed, but she suspected it was around the time she'd stopped thinking about him as His Majesty the King of Ardena and started seeing him as Dante Romero.

Because she knew now that he wasn't just a ruler, he was a man. And while he was undoubtedly handsome and charming and smart and sexy, he was more than that. He was a man she liked and admired. She enjoyed spending time with him, she respected the sharpness of his mind and the warmth of his heart and she seriously lusted after his body.

Okay, so there could be some definite benefits to letting the king put a ring on her finger. But would he want to put a ring on her finger if he knew about her one-night love affair?

"Not tonight," she finally responded to his suggestion.

"You didn't say no this time," he mused. "Maybe next time you'll actually say yes."

Marissa danced with several other people after that, including Dr. Kalidindi, who used the excuse of a fox-trot to press his case. He was as charming as he was persistent, and at the end of their three minutes on the dance floor she found herself agreeing to at least stay another week so that she could tour the pediatric wing of the hospital and meet with him.

When she finally made her way off of the dance floor, she decided to steal a quiet moment alone and catch a breath of fresh air. As guests had been coming and going through the main doors, she opted to slip out of the side entrance for a little privacy.

Apparently she wasn't the only one with that idea, as she saw that Dante had gone out this way, too. Well, she figured it was as good a time as any to tell him that she was staying in Ardena—at least for another week.

It wasn't until he turned to speak to someone that she realized he wasn't alone. She paused with her hand on the glass, her heart hammering in her chest.

She couldn't see who he was with, but he looked angry. Furious. Then his companion stepped into the light, and Marissa sucked in a breath as she recognized the girl who had introduced herself as Naomi when she met her at the hospital in Port Augustine.

She pushed open the door, just a little, unashamedly eavesdropping. They were too far away for her to hear their words, but Dante's tone was harsh, the girl's softer, almost taunting.

Maybe Naomi did know some of the king's secrets—or maybe she *was* one of his secrets. The possibility made Marissa's stomach churn.

No—if Naomi had been sleeping with the king, she would have said so. She'd only told Marissa to ask him about Siobhan, and then she'd refused to say anything more.

It's not my story to tell.

Then whose story was it?

Marissa decided it was time she got an answer to that question.

After their dance, Dante and Marissa went in opposite directions. As much as he wished he could spend all of his time with her, he understood the expectations and protocols of his position. But by midnight, the crowd had thinned considerably and they were finally able to head back to the palace.

He was going to suggest opening a bottle of champagne to toast to the success of the evening, but noticed that she was rubbing her forehead.

"Ready to call it a night?" he asked.

She surprised him by shaking her head. "Actually, I think I'm going to go out back to get some air."

"Do you want company?"

"It's your palace," she reminded him.

Not the most gracious invitation he'd ever received, but he was willing to take it.

She settled in one of the chairs facing the pool, and he chose the one beside her.

"I figured you'd be exhausted after all the work you did—not just today and tonight, but over the past few weeks."

"I am exhausted," she admitted. "But too wired to sleep just yet."

"Anything in particular on your mind?"

"A few things."

He wondered if one of those things was his proposal—or at least the offer from Dr. Kalidindi. "Which one is responsible for that little crease between your brows?"

She shifted her chair so that she was facing him more directly before she responded. "Siobhan."

He looked startled. "What do you know about her?" he asked cautiously.

"I don't know anything," she admitted. "I was hoping you would tell me."

If it was true that she didn't know anything, he could keep the details sparse, giving her enough information to satisfy her curiosity and nothing more. Except that she was looking at him with such unguarded faith that he knew no half-truths would suffice. She was trusting him to tell her the truth; he could only hope that she would believe him when he did.

"Siobhan is the six-month-old daughter of Fiona Breslin, a part-time assistant events coordinator here at the palace. When she was born, she seemed to be a normal, healthy baby, but after a few weeks, Fiona noticed that the infant was struggling to catch her breath and her skin had a slightly bluish tinge."

"She had a hole in her heart," Marissa guessed.

"You obviously spend *a lot* of time at the hospital."

She shook her head. "Gabriella's daughter, Sierra, was born with an atrial septal defect."

"Well, an echocardiogram confirmed that it was an ASD, and while Siobhan's doctor kept promising Fiona that the hole would close on its own, her condition continued to worsen. She finally took her to the hospital, where it was determined that she needed emergency surgery. Unfortunately, there wasn't a surgeon at Mercy qualified to perform that kind of surgery on an infant."

"You sent her to PACH," Marissa realized. "I remember when she was brought in—just a few weeks ago. Dr. Nardone did the surgery."

"And now Siobhan is recovering on schedule."

"There has to be more to the story," she guessed.

He nodded. "As a part-time employee, Fiona had limited medical insurance that didn't cover the cost of transportation to, or any kind of procedure in, a foreign country. It was Fiona's sister, Naomi, who came to me. She said that I had to help, because if I didn't, my baby was going to die."

Marissa's gaze never flickered, never wavered.

"You're not going to ask if it's true—if the baby is mine?"

She shook her head. "I know it's not."

He was as surprised as he was touched by her unquestioning support. "While I appreciate your vote of confidence, how can you be so sure?"

"Because you date supermodels and movie stars—women who, while not of equivalent rank to a king, would be able to relate to you on somewhat equal terms. You would never sleep with someone who worked for you, however indirectly, because of the disparity in your positions. And if I'm wrong about that and you did get involved with an employee, you would never abdicate your responsibilities."

"Well, Fiona didn't know that about me, and apparently— though our paths only crossed on an infrequent basis—she developed something of an infatuation with me."

"She would be one of the half of the women in this country who would give almost anything for the opportunity to be held in your arms?" she teased.

He smiled, appreciating her attempt to lighten the conversation.

"But since that wasn't happening, she hooked up with someone else. And when she found out she was pregnant, she was too ashamed to admit to her sister that the father of her baby abandoned her, so she told her that I was the father."

"An allegation easy enough to disprove," Marissa reminded him.

"But not without a whole lot of publicity and fanfare. And it wasn't just that I didn't want the press speculating that I might have fathered a child out of wedlock and all the issues that went along with that. I didn't want to refocus attention on the funding problem at the hospital, which may or may not have resulted in the baby's condition not being diagnosed properly and treated sooner."

"You covered the cost of Siobhan's medical care, didn't you?"

He nodded. "And maybe that was a mistake, because Naomi interpreted that as proof I felt responsible for the baby and assumed it meant the baby was mine."

"But if you hadn't stepped in, she would have died."

And that was all he'd thought about at the time. He hadn't considered the implications of his actions beyond the fact that they were necessary to save the life of a child.

"So what does she want from you now?" Marissa asked.

"Who?"

"Naomi. I saw her with you at the hotel."

"She doesn't want anything from me. It seems her sole purpose in life, now that her sister's baby is home, is to expose my true character to the people of Ardena, to prove I'm unworthy of wearing the crown."

Marissa reached across the space that separated them and took his hands. "Then you shouldn't worry—because if the people of Ardena see you for who you really are, they'll know how lucky they are to have you as their king."

Her words were a balm to his bruised confidence. "They'd be more likely to believe that if they had a queen who believed it, too."

She only smiled as she released his hands. "Good night, Your Majesty."

He stood with her. "Am I wrong in thinking that we've become friends over the past few weeks, Your Highness?"

"I don't think so," she replied.

"Then maybe you could call me Dante instead of using my title all of the time?"

She nodded. "Good night, Dante."

Nearly a week had passed since the auction and Marissa had yet to make definite plans for her return to Tesoro del Mar. She'd thought she would be eager to get back, and she did miss her family and her friends and the routines at PACH that had become so much a part of her life over the past several years. But whenever she thought about saying goodbye to Dante, she felt an unexpected pang deep inside her heart.

So for now, she was content to maintain the status quo and keep in touch with her family through phone calls and emails. She was at the computer now, and smiling as she read the latest update from Sierra, who was having the time of her life at the University of San Pedro. Marissa finished reading and had just clicked Reply when a quick knock sounded on the door.

Before she had a chance to say anything, the handle turned and Dante walked in. In the six days that had passed since the auction, she'd hardly seen him at all. But suddenly he was here and, without any explanation or apology for his intrusion, he crossed the room to where she was seated at the desk and closed the lid on her laptop.

She lifted her brows. "What are you doing?"

"I'm breaking you out of here," he told her.

"I didn't realize I was being held prisoner."

"Well, I assumed you must be, since you haven't stepped foot outside of the gates of the palace in the past six days, except to visit Dr. Kalidindi."

"Maybe because I haven't wanted to step foot outside of the gates," she suggested.

"I know you don't like being hounded by the media—that's why I brought these." He tossed a neatly folded bundle of clothes on the settee.

"Where did you get those?"

"I pilfered them from Leticia's wardrobe," he explained. "We're going incognito."

She sorted through the items. "How are a pair of jeans, a sweatshirt and a baseball cap going to help me blend in?"

"They're not going to help you blend. Princess Marissa blends. Your disguise is *not* to blend."

"You're kidding."

"Nope." He started toward the door. "I'm giving you five minutes to change, then we're out of here."

"But I was—"

"Four minutes and fifty-five seconds."

She scowled at the back of the door.

After six days of almost no communication, what gave him the right to barge in and start issuing orders? Okay, maybe he was the king of Ardena, but he wasn't the boss of her. And even if she was admittedly curious about his plans, she wasn't going to jump just because he told her to. Not until she was ready.

She opened the lid of her computer again and typed her response to Sierra. When she'd finished her message, she surveyed the borrowed outfit again.

Leticia was of similar height and build to Marissa, but her taste in clothes was very different. Marissa eyed the boldly printed T-shirt, cherry-red hoodie and low-cut dark wash jeans with skepticism. Although she didn't wear them often, she did have jeans of her own—softly faded and conservatively cut—and she was more than a little tempted to dig them out of her drawer instead of wearing Leticia's. But she knew the bundle of clothes Dante had borrowed from his sister wasn't just a commentary on her wardrobe but a challenge, and Marissa never liked to back down from a challenge.

She carried the bundle into the adjoining bedroom and stripped off her skirt and blouse.

Dante paused in the open doorway of Marissa's bedroom, his jaw on the carpet.

He'd counted down the promised five minutes and, assuming that she'd had plenty of time to perform a simple change of clothes, knocked on the door of her sitting room and walked in. But she wasn't in the sitting room—and she hadn't closed the door that separated it from the bedroom.

And she was naked—well, naked except for a couple of scraps of very sexy red lace.

She had her back to him, presenting him with a spectacular view of strong shoulders, slender torso, deliciously curved buttocks and mile-long legs. He swallowed, trying to unstick his tongue from the roof of his mouth to say something. Not that he would be able to speak any coherent words, because the only thought going through his mind was *ohmylordthere-isagodinheaven.*

She bent over to pick up the jeans that she'd laid out on the foot of the bed and his blood roared in his head. She put one foot in, then the other, then she wriggled her hips as she slid the denim up those long, lean legs.

"I know I didn't get those undergarments from my sister's closet."

Marissa yelped and spun around, her eyes wide.

Dante grabbed hold of the doorjamb for support, because as glorious as the view had been of her backside, the front—where delicate cups of scarlet lace cradled unexpectedly lush breasts—was even better.

She grabbed for the T-shirt on the bed, holding it in front of her like a shield. But it was too late—the image of her gorgeous, mostly naked body was already imprinted on his brain forever.

"Don't you knock?" she demanded.

"I told you I would give you five minutes, and your five minutes are up."

"That doesn't give you the right to barge in here!"

"You're right," he admitted.

"Could you please stop staring?" she snapped.

He managed to clear his throat, though he couldn't tear his gaze away. "I honestly don't think I can."

"Dante…"

"Yes?"

"Get out!"

Marissa sank onto the edge of the mattress when he was gone, her heart pounding, her knees weak. She might have succeeded in banishing Dante from her room, but cooling the heat in her veins proved to be a much more challenging task.

With a groan of purely sexual frustration, she yanked the T-shirt over her head, shoved her arms in the sleeves of the sweater and slapped the ball cap on top of her head.

She didn't feel any better when she was done, but at least she was dressed.

He hadn't made a move toward her. He'd just stood in the doorway, more than three feet away. But she'd felt the hunger in his gaze as it raked over her—as tangible as a caress. All it had taken was a look, and everything inside of her had trembled. With awareness. Desire. Need.

It made her wonder what might have happened if he'd actually touched her—just the lightest touch of his fingertips on her skin. Or kissed her—the barest brush of his mouth against hers. No doubt her body would have gone up in flames.

And no way would she be alone on this big, soft bed right now.

Chapter Eleven

Marissa laughed when she saw the beat-up old Volkswagen parked in the underground garage. "We're going out in that?"

"This was my very first car," Dante told her. "And the only one in the garage guaranteed to attract no attention from the paparazzi."

"I can't imagine why."

"But as further insurance that we won't be followed, Thomas just drove through the front gates, headed toward the art gallery. It's a popular tourist destination and the type of cultural experience a visiting princess would certainly enjoy."

"I take it we're not going to the art gallery."

"No, we're not," he confirmed.

But he didn't tell her where they were going.

It was only because she was watching the scenery outside of the window and noticed the recurring signs that she realized he was taking her to Messini National Park.

When she decided to make the trip to Ardena, she'd done some research on the country and had been fascinated by the descriptions of the rocky terrain and the abundance of flora and fauna that existed there.

"We are going to commune with nature," he finally said as he pulled into a completely empty parking lot.

"Hiking the gorge," she guessed. She glanced down at the tennis shoes on her feet with some trepidation.

"It's more of a walk than a hike," he told her, seeming to anticipate her concern. "Other than the first half a kilometer, which is steep, the rest is relatively flat and fairly easy to navigate, so your footwear should be fine."

"How long is this walk?" she wondered.

"It shouldn't take more than a couple of hours, to go through and back again. Maybe less, since we shouldn't have any crowds to contend with."

"I thought I read that this was a popular sightseeing destination. Did you issue some kind of royal decree to get rid of all the tourists?"

"I wish that was an option," he said. "But the truth is, it's only ever really busy during the height of tourist season— between early June and late September," he told her. "Which is why I've always preferred to come early in the spring or late in the fall. Not just to avoid the crowds of visitors scaring away the wildlife, but because the temperature is more moderate."

He opened the hatchback and pulled out a backpack. "Water, power bars, blanket, flashlight, first-aid kit," he explained. "Just in case."

There was only one other vehicle near the start of the trail, so Marissa figured it was a safe bet that they had eluded the paparazzi and let herself relax and enjoy the fresh air and stunning view. He was right about the beginning of the trail—it was steep and comprised mostly of loose rocks, causing her to almost lose her footing once or twice. The first time, Dante grabbed her elbow to steady her. After the second time, he took her hand. And even when the trail leveled out, he kept hold of it.

Their conversation was mostly casual and sporadic, and Marissa found she genuinely enjoyed just being with him, walking along and holding his hand. After an hour, they were almost at the end of the gorge, so Dante suggested they pause to catch their breath. He shrugged the backpack off of his shoulder and took out two bottles of water, passing one to her.

"What do you think?"

"It's incredible," she said, and meant it.

He smiled. "I thought you would like it out here."

"I didn't realize you would," she admitted. "You don't strike me as the outdoorsy type."

"Why's that?"

"Because you look really good in a suit."

He grinned. "You think so?"

"As if you haven't been told that a thousand times before," she remarked drily.

"But never by you."

"I didn't figure your ego needed the stroking." A glimpse of movement caught the corner of her eye and her breath stalled.

"Maybe not my ego," he was saying, "but—"

She reached out and grabbed his arm.

"That's not actually the body part I was thinking about, either."

She glared at him and dropped her voice to a whisper. "What is that?"

He followed the direction of her finger, smiling when he saw what she was pointing at. "A wild goat."

Her hand dropped from his arm. "Those horns are huge."

"You can tell his age by the number of knobs that run up

the length of the horn," he explained. "If you want to get close enough."

"I'll pass."

He chuckled. "It's not likely he'd let you get that close, anyway."

Marissa kept her eyes on the goat—partly because she was fascinated by it but mostly to ensure it maintained a safe distance—until it scampered away.

"This is one of the greatest perks of my job," he said to her.

"Wild goats?"

"Being the boss," he amended. "And being able to sneak out early on a Friday afternoon to spend a few hours in the company of a beautiful woman."

Though her cheeks warmed with pleasure at the compliment, she knew it was a line he'd probably spoken to a lot of women before her. "Well, you are the expert on women."

He gave her a reproachful look as he reached for her hand again. "How are we ever going to make plans for our future if you keep throwing the past in my face?"

"Is it the past?"

"Absolutely," he assured her. "The citizens of Ardena might tolerate a playboy prince but they would never approve of a philandering king."

"But if that king is seen in the company of the 'Prim Princess,' it would go a long way toward restoring his approval rating, wouldn't it?"

"I've never understood that nickname," he said. "Now that I've seen your underwear, I understand it even less. And I find it curious that a woman whose wardrobe is so deliberately bland would favor lingerie that is anything but."

"If you must know, I'm usually a white-cotton kind of girl," she said, her cheeks a bit flushed. "But that set was on sale the last time I was in London."

"I think you're lying."

"Fifty percent off," she said.

"I meant about the white cotton."

Maybe she was lying, but it was a little unnerving that he could read her so easily. She blew out a frustrated breath. "Could we forget about my underwear for five minutes?"

He grinned. "Absolutely not."

She used her free hand to smack him in the chest.

"Assaulting the king is a capital offense," he warned.

"Ardena doesn't have capital punishment."

"I could change that."

"But you wouldn't."

"How do you know?"

"Because you have too much respect for your people to wield your power arbitrarily."

"That's quite the vote of confidence from someone who's only known me a few weeks."

"You're right," she acknowledged. "But I haven't seen any evidence that would contradict it."

"I threatened to fire the chef this morning because he gave me turkey bacon instead of regular bacon with my eggs."

"It's not really a threat if the person on the receiving end knows there's no possibility of follow-through."

"Why are you so sure that I wouldn't fire him?"

"Because he's been cooking your eggs since the days when you ate them soft-boiled with toasted soldiers."

He scowled. "How do you know this stuff?"

She smiled. "I talk to people."

"You mean you use your charm to wheedle secrets out of people."

"I hardly think your breakfast menu is a matter of national security."

"Maybe not," he allowed. "But do you draw a line in your questioning? Is anything off-limits?"

"For now, that will remain *my* secret."

"Do you have many secrets, Your Highness?"

"Not many," she denied. "Although there is something... I don't know if it's really a secret so much as something you should know."

"What's that?"

She stopped and turned so that she was facing him. She worried that it might be a mistake to tell him the truth, but knew it was a bigger mistake not to. She couldn't continue with this charade, allowing the king to think they might have a future together. So she blurted out. "I'm not a virgin."

He seemed to mull over her statement for a minute, then he nodded and resumed walking. "Neither am I."

She fell into step beside him again. "I can't say I'm absolutely shocked by that revelation."

"Did you think I would be shocked by yours?"

"I thought you probably had certain expectations."

"Because a king is expected to marry a woman of noble birth and pure virtue?"

She nodded.

"Expectations have changed since that law was written in the eighteenth century," he told her.

"It really doesn't matter to you?"

"It would be hypocritical of me if it did," he said. "Although I do have one question."

She looked up at him.

"Why are we having this conversation here and now?"

"I figured the middle of the gorge was a safer venue than in my bedroom when I was only half-dressed."

His eyes darkened; his lips curved. "Good point. Because if I'd known then what I know now, we might not have left the palace."

She didn't doubt that was a distinct possibility, and part of the reason that she'd felt compelled to make her confession.

Because as much as she wanted to experience making love with Dante, she was also terrified of that experience. He'd been with a lot of women, women undoubtedly much more knowledgeable and skilled in the bedroom than she, and if and when they did take that next step, she wanted to ensure that his expectations weren't too high.

"I'm not a virgin," she said again. "But I don't have a lot of sexual experience, and—"

"I don't need to hear about your past lovers."

"Lover—singular." She felt her cheeks flush as she made the confession. "There's only been one."

"It doesn't matter," he said. "Because when we make love, you won't think about anyone but me, and you won't remember anyone's touch but mine."

His tone was filled with arrogance, his eyes dark with promise, and Marissa wanted him to prove those words more than she'd ever wanted anything. But as much as her body yearned, her heart was wary.

When she'd been with Jupiter, she hadn't known enough about what to expect to worry. She hadn't realized that sharing herself with a man could be such an incredible experience. She certainly hadn't expected to feel a real and deep connection when their bodies were joined together. Or a profound sense of loss when she slipped away from his room. He'd been a stranger to her, a man whose face she hadn't seen and whose name she didn't know, and still, in the few hours that they'd been together, he'd somehow managed to steal a little piece of her heart.

She knew Dante, not just the kind of man he was but the type of king he wanted to be. Over the past few weeks, she'd talked with him and laughed with him. She'd listened to his hopes and dreams and ambitions, and she'd shared her own with him in turn. She'd watched him with his parents and siblings, noting the obvious affection and close bond the family shared. She'd seen him in front of the cameras, smiling easily and charming the crowd as he cut ceremonial ribbons or shook hands with visiting diplomats. And she'd seen him when the cameras were gone, with a furrow between his brows because being a king wasn't just about photo ops but hard decisions and tough choices.

During that time, she'd realized one undeniable truth: she didn't just like him, she was starting to fall in love with him. And she was very much afraid that she wouldn't be able to make love with him without falling the rest of the way.

As they made their way back through the gorge, Dante couldn't stop thinking about Marissa's revelation.

Her words had surprised him, partly due to the unexpected timing and bluntness of their delivery, but he wouldn't have said he was shocked by her confession. Although the Princess Royal had been confident that Marissa was "still innocent," he hadn't honestly expected that she was untouched. After all, she was twenty-eight years old and, regardless of the efforts she made to hide it, a beautiful woman.

But the Princess Royal's statement hadn't been inaccurate. Because while Marissa might not be a virgin, she was still, in many ways, an innocent. And it was his awareness of that innocence—conscious or not—that had held his growing desire for her in check over the past few weeks.

The first time he'd kissed her, he'd sensed the initial hesitation in her response. He'd admittedly moved in fast and realized that she might prefer to take things at a slightly slower pace. Unfortunately, patience wasn't one of his virtues. When he saw something he wanted, he tended to go after it—and maybe he'd been surprised to realize that he wanted Marissa, but the desire he felt when he was with her was undeniable.

With her mouth moving so softly and sweetly beneath his, that desire had quickly escalated. He'd deepened the kiss and she'd responded, and the flavor of her passion had shot through his veins like a drug.

When he'd finally ended the kiss, he'd seen the reflection of his own wants and needs in the depths of those golden eyes. But hovering beyind the edges of her arousal were hints of something that suggested she was just a little bit afraid.

So he'd ordered himself to take a step back, to give her the time he sensed she needed, to let her set the pace. He'd deliberately kept his touch casual, his flirtation light. And he'd refused to give in to the urge to kiss her again.

But right now, he really wanted to kiss her again.

Thankfully, they were now navigating the steeper part of the trail, and that forced him to focus on something other than his desire for the princess.

"Thank you," she said as they approached the parking lot. "For breaking me out of the palace for a few hours."

"It was my pleasure," he assured her.

"I just hope you don't feel it's your obligation to keep me entertained while I'm here."

He wanted to ask how much longer she planned to stay in Ardena, but he was afraid that if he did, she might get the impression he was anxious for her to go. And nothing could be further from the truth. Instead, he responded teasingly, "Actually, today was about you entertaining me."

"In that case, you're welcome," she said.

"And tomorrow, you get to entertain the whole family."

She halted in midstep. "What does that mean?"

He put his hand on the small of her back, nudging her forward. "It means that my mother has some big meet-the-family dinner planned for tomorrow night."

"I've met your family," she reminded him.

"You met my parents and my siblings. Tomorrow night you'll meet everyone else."

"Who is 'everyone else'?" she wanted to know.

"My grandmothers from both sides, my father's sisters and their husbands and children, my mother's brother, his wife and their daughter."

"Why do I need to meet all of these people?"

"Because you are Princess Marissa of Tesoro del Mar and as soon as they learned you were visiting, they insisted upon an invitation to the palace to meet you."

"What did you tell them about our relationship?" she asked warily, following him back to the car.

"I didn't tell them anything," he assured her. "But I can't vouch for anything my mother may or may not have said."

"I knew coming to Ardena was a bad idea."

"It's dinner with my family, not a press conference."

"I'd rather face a crowd of rabid reporters than a table filled with aunts and uncles and cousins assessing my suitability as a potential royal bride."

"You could put an end to a lot of their questions by letting me put a ring on your finger." He tossed the pack into the back, closed it again.

"I thought you'd given up on that."

"Why would you think that?"

"Well, it wasn't really anything you said or did," she said as he came around to open the passenger door for her. "More like all the things you didn't say or do."

"Such as not kissing you?"

"That's one," she admitted, a hint of pique in her tone.

If only she knew how difficult it had been to keep his distance from her. To resist the urge to kiss her and do all the other things he wanted to do.

"And not leaning close—" he shifted so that his body was angled toward her "—so that I could breathe in your scent when I'm talking to you?"

"I didn't actually think of that one." Her voice was a little softer now, huskier.

"And not touching you—" he traced a fingertip lightly over the line of her collarbone, above the low neckline of her T-shirt "—just for the pleasure of feeling the silky texture of your skin?"

Her eyes drifted shut and her throat moved as she swallowed.

He dipped his head, whispering close to her ear. "And not easing you down onto the middle of your bed to strip those scraps of lace from your body? Tell me, did you think about that one?"

He eased away from her and smiled. The verbal seduction had aroused him unbearably, but he got a little bit of satisfaction from realizing that she was just as aroused as he was.

She blew out a long, slow breath. "I am sooo out of my league with you."

"You wouldn't say that if you knew how twisted up inside I am with wanting you."

Her lips curved. "Really?"

"I promise you, Marissa, my reasons for not doing any or all of those things has absolutely nothing to do with a lack of desire."

"Then...why?"

"Because I don't just want you in my bed—I want you in my life. And I've realized it's not fair to use the attraction between us to put pressure you. So I'm backing off until you decide to give me an answer to my proposal."

"Are you actually refusing to have sex with me until I agree to marry you?"

"Let's just say I'm giving you time."

"What if I don't want time?"

"What do you want?"

She tipped her head back to meet his gaze. "For starters, I want a proper proposal."

His heart actually missed a beat. "Are you going to say yes?"

"It's not a proper proposal if you're not sweating the answer to the question," she informed him.

So he reached into his pocket and then, right there in the middle of the parking lot, he got down on one knee—and watched the princess's jaw drop. He took her hand, felt her fingers tremble in his.

"Marissa Leandres, will you do me the honor of becoming my wife and the queen of Ardena?"

"You have a ring." She said it in the same slightly terrified tone of voice that she might have used to say "you have a gun" if she'd found one was pointed at her.

"Of course I have a ring," he told her. "It's a little difficult to propose without one."

"I can't believe you had a ring. In your pocket. The whole time we were hiking the gorge."

"Actually, I've been carrying it around with me for about a week now, trusting that you would eventually come to your senses."

Her brows lifted. "I wouldn't make any assumptions about my senses, considering that I haven't yet answered your question."

"Well, maybe you could get around to that," he prompted. "These stones are tough on the knees."

She reached for his other hand and drew him to his feet. "Yes, Dante Romero, king of Ardena, I will marry you."

He slid the ring on her finger.

She slid her arms around his neck and lifted her mouth to his. "Now take me home and take me to bed."

He grinned. "Your wish is my command, Your Highness."

Chapter Twelve

Unfortunately, their plans hit a snag when they got back to the palace and found the driveway was crowded with vehicles and the parlor filled with people.

"You told me the party was tomorrow." Marissa's voice was a frantic whisper.

"Because my mother told me the party was tomorrow." Dante also kept his voice low as they hurried through the foyer, hoping to avoid being seen by any of the guests.

But they didn't avoid his mother.

"There you are." Arianna caught them at the foot of the stairs. "I thought I might have to call to summon you home."

If she was surprised by the princess's casual—and borrowed—attire, she didn't show it. She only smiled at Marissa. "The guest of honor shouldn't be late for her own party."

"You said the party was tomorrow," Dante reminded her.

"Because I wanted to surprise you both," the queen said,

unaffected by the reproach in his tone. Because while he might be the king of Ardena, he was still her son.

"Well, as it turns out, I have a surprise, too."

"Oh?" Arianna's gaze automatically dropped to Marissa's left hand, but Dante held it in his own so that the ring on her finger remained out of sight—at least for the moment.

"But we're both sweaty and dusty after a trek through the gorge, so we'd like some time to freshen up."

"Of course," his mother agreed. "But don't take too long. Hors d'oeuvres will be served in less than an hour."

Dante and Marissa started up the stairs as Arianna went back to the party.

"So much for my plan to ignore the crowd and sneak you up to my room," he lamented.

She wasn't entirely sure if he was joking. "Would you really have taken me up to your room with all these people here?"

He paused at the top of the landing and slid his arm around her waist to draw her close. "Princess, I would have taken you in the backseat of that beat-up old car if I'd known we'd be coming back to a full house." His lips twisted in a wry smile. "My own fault, I guess, for wanting something more memorable and comfortable than cracked vinyl upholstery."

"It would have been memorable for me," she said. "I've never done it in the back of a car."

"Neither have I," he admitted. "But it wasn't how I envisioned celebrating our engagement."

"Well—" she slid her palms up his chest and over his shoulders to link them behind his neck "—your mom did give us almost an hour."

"Trust me, Princess, the first time I make love with you, it's going to take a lot more time than that."

"You keep making these promises and I have yet to see any evidence of follow-through."

The glint in his eyes was sexy, determined and just a little bit dangerous, and it sent shivers of anticipation dancing down her spine.

"Screw the party," he decided, reaching for the handle of her door.

Then muttered a curse when the sound of a throat being cleared, deliberately and loudly, came from down the hall.

Marissa had to laugh, though she really wanted to scream in expression of her own frustration. "Does it feel as if the world is conspiring against us?"

"Not the world, just my family," he grumbled as Francesca drew nearer.

"Mother sent me up on the pretext of checking to see if Marissa needed any help getting ready."

"And the real reason?" Dante asked.

His sister grinned. "I think she's afraid that the king will try to sneak some alone time with the princess." Her eyes went wide as she caught sight of the ring. "Or should I say his bride-to-be?"

"Oh. Um." Marissa looked at Dante, not quite sure what to say and afraid she'd broken some sort of protocol by letting his sister see the ring before he'd told his parents of their engagement.

"It's great-grandmother's ring," Francesca murmured, then looked to her brother for confirmation.

Dante only gave a brief nod.

"But you said—"

"That I couldn't take great-grandmother's ring until I'd found the right woman to give it to," he concluded for her.

His sister turned her attention back to Marissa. "Has my mother seen it?"

"We haven't told anyone yet," she said.

"I won't let on that I was the first to know," Francesca promised. Then she kissed both of Marissa's cheeks before turning to kiss her brother's cheeks, too. "I'm so happy for both of you."

"We'd be happy, too, if you'd get lost for a while," Dante told her.

His sister shook her head, almost regretfully. "If I go back downstairs, she'll just send Leticia or maybe even come up herself."

"You're right," he acknowledged. Then he turned his back on her and kissed Marissa softly, deeply. "Later."

Later seemed to be a very long time in coming.

What Arianna had promised would be a simple dinner party to introduce Marissa to the rest of the family turned into an impromptu celebration of their engagement, and it seemed as if none of the guests ever intended to go home.

And then, to the collective surprise of everyone gathered, the butler entered the room to announce the arrival of another guest.

"Her Royal Highness, the Princess Royal Elena Leandres of Tesoro del Mar."

Three hours later, Marissa still wasn't sure what had precipitated her mother's impromptu trip to Ardena. But at least the Princess Royal seemed to be behaving herself—sipping brandy and chatting amiably with the other guests.

"It's my fault," Dante admitted when she confessed she was at a complete loss to explain her mother's sudden and unexpected arrival.

"What did you do?"

"I called and told her that we were engaged because I didn't want her to read about it in the paper."

Which was both a sweet and thoughtful gesture, but she had to ask, "Couldn't you have at least waited until morning?"

"I could and should have," he agreed. "And I would have

if I'd known she had some weird kind of maternal radar that made her show up before you could sacrifice your virtue outside of wedlock."

She laughed at the thought. "My mother doesn't have a motherly bone—never mind anything else maternal—in her body."

"But maybe she's right," he said.

The quiet resignation in his tone made her wary. "About what?"

"Wanting you to wait."

"She wants me to wait because she thinks I'm a virgin," Marissa reminded him.

"And you're not," he acknowledged.

"Right, so there's no reason for us to wait."

"Except that you've only ever been with one man."

She was completely baffled by his response. "So?"

"So he must have been someone you really cared about."

He was wrong. In fact, he was so far off base she might have laughed if she didn't feel so much like crying. Hannah was right—Marissa never should have given her virginity to a stranger. She should have waited, not necessarily to fall in love but at least to be with someone she liked, someone she truly cared about. Someone like Dante.

She could tell him the truth—that her lover had been a stranger, a man whose name—and face—she didn't even know, a one-night stand. But if she told him that, would he look at her with censure instead of respect? Would he decide that a woman who could give her virginity away so easily wasn't a suitable bride, after all?

"First you didn't want to sleep with me until I'd made a decision about your proposal, now you want to wait until we're married?"

"I just can't see it happening with your mother looking over my shoulder—figuratively speaking."

"I'll make sure she's on a plane back to Tesoro del Mar by tomorrow."

"But just in case she isn't that easy to get rid of, let's set a date."

"For sex?"

"And I thought I had a one-track mind," he said, shaking his head. "No, I meant for the wedding."

"June," she said, because she'd always imagined that she would one day be a June bride.

"I was thinking December."

She stared at him. "As in two months from now?"

"Sure. Two months from today," he agreed.

"Are you kidding? We can't possibly plan a wedding in two months."

"Probably not," he agreed. "Which is why we'll delegate."

And so their wedding date was set for December twenty-first, because Dante thought their wedding would be a perfect way to start the holiday celebrations.

Arianna and Benedicto weren't surprised that Dante and Marissa wanted a short engagement, but they were surprised by how very short it would be. Elena, on the other hand, didn't seem at all bothered by the narrow time frame. No doubt she knew that the wedding, and consequently all of the planning, would take place in Ardena, so all that would be expected of her was to greet the guests as the mother of the bride.

Still, Marissa thought she would want to be involved in making the arrangements, and when she went to her mother's room Monday morning, she didn't expect to see the Princess Royal's suitcases packed and ready to go. "You're leaving already?"

"There's really no reason for me to stay any longer," Elena said. "You're going to be busy deciding on flowers and menus and cakes—all the kind of details that you always handle so well—and I've got appointments and meetings to attend to at home."

Marissa wasn't disappointed that her mother wasn't staying, but she was disappointed that Elena didn't seem more interested in her only daughter's wedding. And then she recognized a truth that had been nudging at the back of her mind since the Princess Royal had shown up the night of her engagement to Dante.

"You didn't really come here for me," she said to her mother. "You just used the engagement as an excuse to see Benedicto."

For a moment—maybe just half a second—Marissa thought she caught a glimpse of genuine emotion flicker in her mother's eyes. But it was just a glimpse, and it was gone before she could begin to decipher what it might have been.

"I was…curious," Elena admitted. "I hadn't seen him in a very long time."

"Why didn't you ever tell me that you knew him?"

"It didn't seem relevant."

"The father of my fiancé was almost your fiancé, and you didn't think that piece of information was relevant?"

"As I said, it was a long time ago."

"He said that he was going to marry you."

"No formal arrangements had been made."

The confirmation wasn't unexpected, and still Marissa couldn't seem to put all of the pieces together. At least not in any way that made sense to her.

"You could have been the queen of Ardena."

And she couldn't imagine anything that would have made her mother happier. She'd had a chance to step into the spotlight—to marry the man who would be king, to stand beside him as his queen—and she'd turned it down.

"Yes, I could have been," Elena agreed, but offered no further information or explanation.

Marissa found herself thinking of Arianna, the woman who had married Benedicto, become his wife and his queen and the mother of his children. A woman who loved her family and enjoyed spending time with them, who smiled frequently and laughed easily, who was not just content but truly happy with her life. A woman who was undoubtedly aware of the history between her husband and her future daughter-in-law's mother and had still graciously opened up her home to the other woman.

Elena, by contrast, never seemed content. No matter what she had, it was never what she wanted; no matter how much she had, it was never enough. Marissa had never stopped hoping that her mother would find happiness somewhere, but she was beginning to despair of that ever happening.

"Did you love him?" she asked her mother now.

Elena considered her answer for a moment before replying, "I loved the idea of marrying a man who would someday be king."

Which was, Marissa realized with a combination of acceptance and disappointment, exactly the response she should have expected from her mother. And yet, it didn't explain why Elena had refused a marriage that would have given her everything she wanted.

"But even more than I wanted to be queen," she continued, "I wanted my father to know that I could make my own choices."

"And yet, you had no reservation about making mine for me," Marissa noted.

"Because I wanted you to make a better choice than the one I had made."

"How did you end up with my father?"

"A chance meeting, a physical attraction." Elena's lips

curved, just a little, in response to the memory. "He was big and strong and so incredibly, ruggedly handsome. Just looking at him made my heart pound and my knees weak.

"But reality has a way of dulling the brilliant shine of a new romance, and when I discovered I was pregnant with Michael and he insisted that we should get married, I panicked."

"You were pregnant before you got married?" Marissa had never been privy to that little detail, and she was shocked that Elena would reveal it now.

"Disgraceful, isn't it?" Her mother actually smiled, as if pleased to have been involved in such a scandal. "But as thrilling as it was to have a passionate affair with a farmer, I knew it wouldn't be nearly as exciting to be the wife of a commoner. So I planned to seduce Benedicto and tell him that the baby was his."

Marissa couldn't hold back her shocked gasp.

"But before I could put my plan into action, Gaetan showed up at the palace," Elena continued. "He told my father that I was pregnant and that he wanted to marry me. Prince Emmanuel was furious."

Elena blinked and Marissa thought she caught a glimpse of moisture in her eyes, but when the Princess Royal looked at her daughter again, her face was composed.

"He kicked me out," she said matter-of-factly. "And he told me that if I married the father of my baby, I would keep my title and my inheritance. But if I refused, he would disown me."

Marissa winced, imagining how those cruel words would have stabbed through Elena's fragile heart. Maybe she'd been impulsive and reckless, but she'd been young and desperately seeking her father's attention, and Marissa couldn't help but think that the seeds of her mother's present unhappiness might have been sown by her father's rejection on that long-ago day.

"So I married Gaetan," Elena concluded. "And the country priest was persuaded, by a sizable donation to the church coffers, to backdate the certificate so that no one would raise an eyebrow when a child was born less than eight months after our wedding.

"And then Cameron was born two years after that and, as far as I was concerned, I'd fulfilled my wifely obligations to my husband," Elena said. "I'd borne him two sons and had no intention of going through pregnancy and childbirth again.

"But he persuaded me to try once more, because he wanted a little girl. And from the moment you were born, you were his princess. Even if you hadn't been one by blood, you would have been one in his eyes."

Marissa felt the sting of tears in her eyes. "I barely even remember him," she admitted softly.

"He was a good man," Elena told her. "And a great father."

"But you didn't love him," she realized.

Her mother shook her head. "Not the way he deserved to be loved," she admitted. "And not the way he loved me."

"But you stayed with him."

"I'd made my choice, and if my life wasn't everything I'd hoped it might be, I had no one to blame but myself," she explained. "I still don't know if it was right or wrong, but I can't deny that I've often wondered how different things might have been if I'd walked away from Gaetan instead of toward him. And if it seems as if I pushed you into Dante's arms, it's because I didn't want you to make the same mistakes I did.

"Maybe an arranged marriage to the king of Ardena isn't the fairy-tale romance you've dreamed of, but the reality is that, regardless of whom you marry, you will be stuck under the same roof with him for the rest of your life. And I guarantee you that the roof of a palace will afford you much more freedom than that of a three-bedroom farmhouse in the middle of nowhere."

Marissa didn't doubt that was true. But she'd gladly live in a farmhouse in the middle of nowhere if she knew that she was loved. Instead, she was preparing for her holiday wedding to the man she loved with no idea if he would ever fall in love with her, too.

The King Finally Chooses His Queen!

That headline—and countless variations of it—was everywhere she turned. The attention Dante and Marissa were getting was ridiculous. Part of that was a result of the world being in love with love, especially when there was a royal romance involved. Since all of the pomp and circumstance surrounding Prince William's wedding to Catherine Middleton, everyone was clamoring for more.

There was no doubt that Ardena's king and the Tesorian princess made a beautiful couple. It would only make it that much more tragic when the esteemed ruler fell from grace. And he would fall—of that she had no doubt.

If His Majesty's conduct was deemed "unbecoming," the King's Council could demand that he abdicate. The provision was one that had never actually been used in Ardena's history, but it was legal and valid, and she was determined to compile all the evidence the council needed to take away Dante Romero's crown.

The presence of Marissa Leandres was a complication she hadn't anticipated. She had no grudge against the Tesorian princess, but she wasn't going to feel guilty if the king's bride-to-be got caught in the crossfire.

After all, she'd been warned.

Chapter Thirteen

Marissa had kept in regular contact with both of her sisters-in-law, via email and telephone, since she'd left Tesoro del Mar. That contact had gone from frequent to daily in the almost two weeks that had passed since Marissa and Dante announced their engagement and the date of their Christmas wedding. So she was neither surprised nor alarmed when her cell rang and she recognized Hannah's number on the display.

The panic didn't start until she heard her say, "You have to get on a plane and get your butt back here now."

"Why? What's wrong?"

"What's wrong is that you made Gabriella promise not to have the baby until you got home, but no one checked to make sure the baby was in agreement with the deal."

Excitement pushed aside the panic. "Gabby's in labor?"

"Her water broke ten minutes ago. The contractions haven't started yet, but—"

"I have to call the airline. I have to get home." While Dante had access to a private jet for business and personal use, she didn't feel comfortable asking for a free ride back to Tesoro del Mar. In any event, commercial flights between the two island nations were frequent enough that she wouldn't have to wait long to get on a plane for the trip home.

"Michael just finished booking your ticket. He's sending the details to your cell phone."

"In that case, I'll see you soon."

She disconnected that call, then dialed Thomas to request a ride to the airport. She figured she would call Dante when she was en route but remembered that he was at a planning meeting. Instead, she grabbed her passport and hurried to the king's private office to write a quick note for him.

Reaching across the desk for a pen, she accidentally knocked his leather-bound agenda off the edge. As she bent to retrieve it, a flash of color caught her eye and her heart jolted.

Between the pages, where the book had fallen open, was a single peacock feather.

She lifted it by the broken end and stroked a finger over the silky face, tracing the outer edge of the eye as questions pounded in her brain.

Could this be the same feather that had broken off of her mask? She didn't know where or when she'd lost the feather, not having discovered that the decoration was missing until she got home in the early hours of the morning after the masquerade ball.

Was it possible that Dante was the man she'd made love with that night? Holding that feather in her hand, she knew it wasn't only possible but true. Dante *was* Jupiter.

Now that she'd put the pieces together, she wondered that she hadn't recognized the truth sooner. The unexpected attraction she'd felt when she first met the king was so eerily similar to the feelings she'd experienced with Jupiter. Not similar—the same. She hadn't been attracted to two different men, because they were the same man.

Bits and pieces of their conversation from that first night filtered through her mind:

Why would I choose the identity of any one god when I could be the ruler of the gods? A logical perspective, now that she understood he was the ruler of his country.

I can't give you anything more than this night. Because he was a king in search of a queen, but distracted from his quest by the magical seduction of the night.

And it explained why he'd been as careful as she to ensure that their encounter remained anonymous. Had he intended it to be one last fling before he found a bride? Or was it his modus operandi? Was he the kind of man who would take any willing woman to his bed? Certainly the tabloids had given him that reputation, and maybe if Marissa had learned of the Jupiter connection a few weeks earlier, she might have been more inclined to believe it.

Or maybe not. Because even that night, when she knew nothing about him and had no clue as to his real identity, he'd been an attentive and considerate lover. Not a man who used women for his own purposes, but one who respected and appreciated them. And when he'd realized that he'd taken her innocence, he'd seemed genuinely remorseful.

...if I'd known you were untouched, I would have made sure you stayed that way.

Why?

Because your first time shouldn't be with a stranger.

Jupiter had asked her if she believed in destiny—she'd told him that she was in control of her destiny. But now, realizing that her lover that night was the man she was going to marry, she acknowledged that there might have been a stronger force at work than her own determination. Maybe she and Dante really were fated to be together.

She'd fallen halfway in love with him that night, without even knowing who he was. And now, knowing everything else that she knew about him, she couldn't help but tumble the rest of the way.

Through the window, she saw Thomas's car coming down the drive. Quickly tucking the feather between the pages again, she closed the book and returned it to its place on his desk.

She left Dante's office, forgetting to write a note.

After almost nine months in office, the new king felt as if he was finally getting the hang of things. Of course, it helped that the men and women who had been his father's most trusted advisers were now his advisers. Under their tutelage, he was making real progress, and even the press was reporting a significant improvement in his approval rating. Or maybe it was just the holidays on the horizon that were responsible for his critics being in a more charitable mood. But the biggest change, from Dante's perspective, was having Marissa in his life.

If he thought about it, it might surprise him how much he looked forward to seeing her at the end of every day. So he tried not to think about it and just enjoy the happiness and contentment he felt when he was with her. Not that he was entirely content, but he knew he only had himself to blame for the status quo.

It had been his decision to wait to consummate their relationship, and it wasn't a decision his fiancée had acceded to willingly. As she continued to remind him by doing everything possible to elevate the level of his frustration. Sliding her hand along his thigh whenever she sat beside him at dinner, rubbing her breast against his arm when she reached for the remote control if they were watching television, letting her lips brush his ear when she whispered to him. And when he kissed her—because he wasn't masochistic enough to cut off all physical contact—she did things with her tongue that nearly made his eyes cross.

She might be an admitted novice at lovemaking, but she was a definite pro at seduction. And with each day that passed, his resistance was waning in direct proportion to his escalating desire. Until he began to wonder why he was fighting against something that he wanted as badly as she did.

By the time he was heading back to his suite Wednesday night, he'd decided to stop fighting and start planning. After all, he wasn't without his own skills when it came to setting a scene for seduction.

He had a definite spring in his step when he set off to find his future queen.

While another office was being renovated for Marissa's future use, he'd suggested that she could work in the office that adjoined his suite, and she often did. But when he peeked in there today, it was empty. He checked her suite next—ensuring that he knocked before he entered, because a man could only handle so much temptation—but she wasn't there, either. He glanced in the library, conservatory, kitchen and pool area, and though there were plenty of staff bustling around as preparations were being made not just for the wedding reception that would be held on-site but for the upcoming holiday season, there was no sign of Marissa.

He went back to his office, only now noticing the large, flat envelope on his desk. There was a neatly printed label on the front with his name and Personal & Confidential in bold print. But there was no postmark, and he instinctively suspected that Naomi was behind whatever was in the envelope.

He was growing tired of her threats. He'd tried to see things from her perspective: she truly believed that he'd seduced her sister then abandoned her when she got pregnant, denying paternity of the baby simply because he was embarrassed to have fathered a child out of wedlock with a commoner. If any part of that scenario had been true, she would have been entitled to her anger and her frustration. But it was all a fabrication, a lie Fiona had made up rather than admit the truth to the little sister who adored her.

He'd been honest with Naomi, but loyalty to her sister had closed her mind to the truth. She'd refused to listen to any version of events that didn't correspond with the story that was set in her mind. His offer to have a paternity test didn't sway her—"the lab techs would say whatever the king wanted them to say." His willingness to cover the costs of not just Siobhan's medical bills but Fiona's travel and living expenses while in Tesoro del Mar didn't soften her—"that's the least you can do for your own child."

He'd confronted Fiona. She'd been embarrassed and ashamed, but she'd owned up to her lies. Unfortunately, her confession to her sister had fallen on deaf ears and Naomi remained convinced that he'd somehow bribed or blackmailed Fiona into changing her story, burying the truth.

If there was one bright light in the whole dark mess, it was that Marissa believed in him. Even before she'd heard the whole story, she'd trusted that he was too honorable and decent to do what Naomi had accused him of doing. And because she believed in him, she made him want to be a better person.

He'd spent his whole life in the spotlight. He was accustomed to attention and adoration. But no one had ever made him feel the way he felt when he was with Marissa.

He opened the flap, then tipped the package so the document would slide out. He almost hoped it was a court application for child support—he'd almost rather go public to clear up the story than continue to live with the cloud of suspicion over his head.

Except that it wasn't a document—it was a collection of photos that spilled out.

Glossy, full-color, eight-by-ten photos.

He sifted through the pictures, his heart pounding hard and fast inside his chest.

The pictures had been taken the night of the Mythos Ball, outside of his room at the palace. Pictures of a man and a woman in period costume and elaborate masks. Jupiter and Juno.

He sifted through the photos. The one on top was a full-body shot. More specifically, Jupiter's body pressing Juno's against the door, their mouths locked together. There were several photos of them kissing. And then the photographer had creatively zoomed and cropped to show a close-up of his tongue touching the bow of her top lip and his hand on her breast.

Naomi had made it her mission to destroy him, and he realized that these pictures might finally do it. He didn't think he would lose the throne. While the publication of the images—if that was what Naomi intended—would hardly be a shining moment for the crown, what had happened that night was nothing more complicated than two consenting adults hooking up for a few hours of mutual pleasure. There was no one who could claim it was anything more nefarious than that.

Unless Naomi had somehow discovered Juno's true identity. Or if—the thought made his blood run cold—she had always known the truth about who Juno was and the whole interlude had been a setup from the beginning.

He buried his face in his hands. Okay, so maybe he was being paranoid. After all, it wasn't as if Juno had approached him—he'd been the one who spotted her, and he'd been the one to invite her back to his room.

Juno had been a fantasy. And for one glorious night, she'd

been his fantasy. Then he'd met Marissa. And he'd discovered that she was better than any fantasy, because she was generous and compassionate and real.

Truthfully, he didn't even care if the people of Ardena wanted to take away his crown as a result of this indiscretion. The only thing that mattered to him was Marissa. He couldn't lose her now. If he did—

He felt as if there was a clamp around his chest, squeezing tight.

No, he wouldn't even consider the possibility.

But what if she'd seen these pictures?

Marissa went straight to the hospital from the airport and managed to arrive a full twenty minutes before Talisa Jaime Leandres entered the world.

Hannah and Michael were already at the hospital when she arrived. While they waited, they talked about weddings and babies and all manner of subjects in between. Or maybe it would be more accurate to say that Marissa and Hannah talked while Michael paced.

And then, finally, Cameron stepped out of the delivery room. He looked bone-tired but was wearing a mile-wide grin. "Who wants to see our beautiful new baby girl?"

Of course they all did, but Marissa let Hannah and Michael lead the way because she knew that they had to be home for Riley when she finished school. After they'd congratulated the parents and oohed and aahed over the baby and promised to come back later with Riley, they slipped out of the room, allowing Marissa her first unobstructed view of the newborn.

"Oh, wow." She felt the sting of tears and a sharp pang of longing as her gaze landed on the perfect little girl swaddled in a pink blanket in her sister-in-law's arms. "She's absolutely gorgeous."

The proud daddy smiled. "She is, isn't she?"

He sounded so smug that Marissa couldn't resist teasing, "Because she looks like her mother."

"I think she has her daddy's nose," Gabby said loyally.

Marissa studied the baby for a minute, then shook her head. "Nope—no sign of her daddy at all."

"And I'm okay with that," Cameron said as he leaned in to kiss his wife. "Because I happen to be married to the most beautiful woman in the world."

"And the fact that you can say that with a straight face so soon after I've given birth proves that you really do love me."

"With all my heart," he promised and brushed his lips against hers again.

Marissa's heart sighed as she watched them.

There had been a time when her brother was one of the most notorious playboys around and she didn't think he would ever change. But from the moment he'd met up with Gabriella again, after almost sixteen years apart, everything had changed. Marissa had been surprised by his apparent transformation, and then she'd realized it wasn't that Cameron had changed, but that he'd finally found the woman he loved.

She wondered if she was foolish to hope that Dante would ever look at her with the same obvious love and devotion she saw in her brother's eyes when he looked at his wife. She knew that Dante's proposal was based on practical and political reasons. Emotion wasn't a factor in the equation, at least not on his side. But she was optimistic that the attraction and affection between them would help them to build a strong and solid marriage. And she did believe that the holidays were a time of miracles, maybe even enough to hope that their Christmas wedding would truly lead to a happily-ever-after.

* * *

Dante had already checked his phone, and while the record showed several missed calls from Marissa, there were no messages. And when he'd dialed her number, his call went directly to voice mail.

Where the heck could she have gone that she would have turned off her phone?

He had picked up the phone to try her number again when it began to ring.

"Marissa?"

"It's a girl," she said, and she sounded so blissfully happy that, for a moment, his mind went blank. "Nearly eight pounds and twenty inches, and absolutely gorgeous."

"You're in Tesoro del Mar," he realized.

"Of course. That's where Gabby was having the baby." And then, as if she'd just realized that he might have been worried to arrive home and find his fiancée had disappeared, she said, "Oh, Dante, I'm so sorry. I went into your office to leave a note, but…I got distracted, and then the car was there to take me to the airport and I completely forgot."

He exhaled a breath he hadn't realized he was holding. She'd been in his office but she hadn't seen the pictures. She hadn't left the palace because she was angry or upset—she left because her sister-in-law was in labor. The knowledge didn't entirely alleviate his concerns, but Marissa's explanation reassured him that there wasn't an immediate crisis.

"It's the baby thing," she said, and he could hear the smile in her voice.

"It's okay," he said, willing to forget his momentary panic now that the vise around his chest had finally eased. But the sticky note scrawled with the words "You will pay" attached to the back of one of the photos continued to worry his mind and weight on his heart.

"I really want a baby, Dante."

"That's hardly a revelation."

"I don't mean that I want a baby at some vague point in the future," she clarified. "I want us to make a baby. Soon."

The idea of procreating had always seemed to Dante like just another of those royal expectations he was required to fulfill. But a baby with Marissa—yeah, he really wanted that.

"It's kind of hard to do long-distance," he warned.

"It's kind of hard to do without making love," she pointed out.

"Then I guess I'll have to let you have your way with me."

"Really?" She sounded as dubious as she did hopeful. "Because so help me, Dante, if you're not serious—"

"I am very serious," he promised her.

"What changed your mind?"

"I looked at the calendar and saw that December twenty-first is too damn far away."

She laughed. "I'll be back at two o'clock on Friday."

"I have meetings all day Friday," he told her, even as he mentally reviewed his schedule to figure out if there were some things that could be moved around.

"Then I guess we'll have to wait until Friday night."

"We could get started sooner if you came back tonight," he suggested, hoping to tempt her, wanting—almost desperately—to hold her in his arms. Because as soon as she got home, he would tell her about the photos, and then he could finally put that night behind him and look forward to his future with Marissa.

"I've got some things to do here tomorrow," she told him.

"They're going to put up the Christmas tree in the foyer tomorrow," he said, hoping her desire to participate in the holiday preparations would convince her to change her plans.

"I'm sorry I'll have to miss that," she said.

He took some solace from the fact that she sounded sincerely regretful and crossed his fingers that Naomi wouldn't make another move until he had a chance to talk to Marissa. Maybe when Naomi threatened to make him pay she was hoping for money, and he would get some kind of blackmail demand before she went public with the photos. And though it chafed to think of giving her anything, he knew he would pay whatever she wanted to keep the pictures out of the media and his fiancée out of the spotlight.

"I miss you already," he told her.

"I've only been gone a few hours."

And he'd been to hell and back in those few hours, trying to figure out where she'd gone and why she'd left him. Of course, he didn't admit any of that to her now. He only said, "I guess I've just become accustomed to having you around."

"Then maybe it's a good thing that I'll be away for a few days. I wouldn't want you to start taking me for granted."

"Never again," he promised and knew that it was true.

If she would only come home, he would spend every day of the rest of their lives showing her how very much she meant to him.

Marissa was eager to get back to Ardena—to get back to Dante. Unlike the first trip she'd taken on the king's private plane, this time she experienced absolutely no apprehension about leaving her home. This time, she felt as if she was going home.

In the almost five weeks that she'd spent in Ardena, she'd quickly grown to appreciate the rugged country and its resilient people. She knew she would miss the staff and her routines at PACH, but she'd found new direction and purpose working with Dr. Kalidindi at Mercy. The entire Romero family had welcomed her from the start—Arianna a little more hesitantly than the rest, but now that Marissa knew of her mother's past with the other woman's husband, she could understand her reservations—and she'd been honored and humbled by their acceptance. She was looking forward to being part of their family, to sharing the holidays and participating in local traditions with them—including the upcoming olive harvest and the Christmas parade. But the most unexpected and thrilling discovery for Marissa was that she'd fallen in love with the man she was going to marry.

She wasn't ready to believe that Dante had fallen in love with her, too, but she was hopeful that it might happen. Someday.

When she exited into the arrivals lounge, she was so intent on searching for the chauffeur that her gaze skipped right past her fiancé. It was actually the two broad-shouldered guards flanking him that she spotted first, and when she realized that Dante was there to meet her, her heart skipped a beat.

She hadn't expected to see him and she was suddenly nervous. She'd only been away three days, but those three days had seemed interminable. She smoothed a hand down the front of her sapphire-colored dress, wondering if he would look at her any differently today and how she would feel if he did.

His gaze skimmed over her slowly, appreciatively, and his lips curved as he made his way toward her.

She curtsied; he bowed; cameras flashed.

"I thought you had meetings all day," she said.

"I managed to clear my schedule so that I could be here to meet you."

His gaze dropped to her mouth, and she knew that he wanted to kiss her. She also knew that he was as conscious of the crowd of onlookers as she, so he only lifted her hand to his lips.

"I didn't expect you to be here," she said, torn between pleasure and guilt. "But it was a thoughtful gesture."

"Not a grand gesture?" he teased, referencing a comment she'd made once before.

"That will depend on the vehicle your chauffeur is driving."

He laughed and offered his arm.

Marissa placed her hand in the crook of his elbow and pretended she didn't notice all of the heads that turned in their direction. There would be more photos in the paper tomorrow and new headlines, but she refused to let it bother her. She might not have completely overcome her wariness of the media, but she'd accepted that there would be very little privacy in her life with the king of Ardena—and she knew that a few stolen moments with Dante would make everything worthwhile.

She smiled when she saw the glossy stretch Bentley waiting for them. "Okay, I'll give you *grand*."

Thomas greeted her with a formal bow and a quick wink as he reached for the handle of the door. Marissa stepped up into the back of the car—and into a veritable greenhouse.

The back of the limo was absolutely filled with flowers. Buckets and buckets overflowing with colorful, fragrant blooms. She had a moment to think it was a good thing the king's bodyguards rode in a separate vehicle because there was no room for them back here.

She skimmed a finger over the velvety-soft petal of a lavender calla lily as Dante settled beside her. "A *very* grand gesture," she amended.

"Flowers are a common element in many courtship rituals," he told her.

"Are you courting me, Your Majesty?"

"Considering that our wedding is only a few weeks away, it seemed like I should fit that in somewhere."

"I appreciate the effort," she assured him, "but you don't have to wine—"

She broke off, laughing as he popped the cork on a bottle of champagne.

"You were saying?" he prompted.

"That you don't need to wine and dine me," she finished, even as she accepted the glass of wine he passed to her.

"Good, because I haven't planned as far ahead as dinner." He tapped the rim of his glass against hers. "Welcome home, Marissa."

And then, finally, he kissed her.

It was a long while later before he said, "I like your dress."

She smiled, pleased that he had noticed. "Hannah and Gabby convinced me that all the beige in the world wouldn't insulate the king's fiancée from public scrutiny, so I decided to show my true colors."

"I like those true colors—just as long as this isn't some kind of wardrobe reversal and now your underwear is white cotton," he said.

She shook her head and whispered, close to his ear, "Purple satin demi-cup bra."

His lips curved. "Matching bikinis?"

She shook her head again and saw the spark of hope fade. "Matching thong."

His eyes glittered with heat and hunger. "You really enjoy torturing me, don't you?"

"Maybe." She shifted so that her lips hovered just a breath away from his. "Just a little."

The limo drew to a stop.

Dante took her hand.

She asked no questions and made no protest as he ushered her toward the double front doors on which hung twin wreaths decorated with gold bows. Inside the foyer was the Christmas tree he'd told her about—it was at least fifteen feet tall and elegantly decorated with gold-and-silver balls and bows. But he didn't give her any time to admire the holiday decor, instead leading her directly upstairs and into his suite.

She held his gaze as he closed the door, her eyes filled with passion and promise as she reached for the tie at the side of her dress. He caught her hands, knowing there was no way he would be able to get a single word out if she unfastened that knot.

"We need to talk."

Marissa's hands dropped to her sides as she looked at him, her expression one of both disappointment and disbelief. "You're telling me that you cleared your schedule this afternoon because you want to talk?"

He let his gaze skim over her again, admiring the way the silky blue fabric of the wrap-style dress molded to her feminine curves and wanting her with a desperation he'd never known before.

"No," he said honestly, his voice husky with desire. "What I want to do is strip you naked and take you to bed and spend hours showing you how much I missed you."

Her lips started to curve.

"But I need to be honest with you about something first."

The smile faded. "That sounds ominous."

He took her hands, squeezed gently. "I hope not."

"Then just say it fast and get it over with."

But somehow he didn't think blurting out that he'd had sex with another woman the night before they met was going to score him any points. So he decided to start his explanation a little closer to the beginning.

"When I went to Tesoro del Mar in September, it was with the intention of asking you to marry me."

"But you didn't even know me then."

"I knew enough," he said. "You once asked if it was one of my assistant's jobs to research the likes and dislikes of my dates. I never went to such lengths for a casual acquaintance, but my advisers felt it was necessary for me to have some basic information about the women who were on the bride list."

Her brows rose. "The bride list?"

"Sorry—that's what my brother Matt dubbed it. But it was a list of women that my advisers decided were the most suitable candidates for marriage."

"And I was on that list because I was a Tesorian princess."

"You were at the top of the list. And I decided that as long as we were reasonably compatible, I wouldn't bother to look any further."

"I'm flattered," she said, though her tone suggested otherwise.

The phone on his desk rang, but Dante ignored it. He wasn't going to allow anything to interrupt his confession, because he knew that Marissa needed to know the truth about the secret in his past before they could look to their future together. And she had to know now. Though he couldn't be certain that the text message he'd received while waiting for Marissa's plane at the airport had been from Naomi, the brief tick tock was clearly a warning that his time was running out.

"I was prepared to marry for duty rather than desire," he admitted. "So I was very pleasantly surprised to discover that there was something more between us, right from the beginning."

He took her left hand, rubbed his thumb over the ring on her third finger. "Do you remember how surprised Francesca was when she realized I'd given you my great-grandmother's ring?"

She nodded.

"My father had offered it to me before I made that trip and I wouldn't take it. Because I couldn't imagine giving a ring that my great-grandfather had given to my great-grandmother, as an expression of his love and affection, to a woman I was marrying only out of obligation."

The cell phone in his pocket vibrated and a trickle of unease worked its way down his spine. But he forged ahead, desperate to tell her the truth, to make her understand.

"I chose to give you that ring because my feelings for you changed, because I fell in love with you. And when I put that ring on your finger, I did so knowing that I would always be faithful to the woman who wore it."

"You…love me?" She sounded so bewildered and she looked up at him with so much love and hope shimmering in her eyes it nearly broke his heart—because he knew that what he was about to tell her might break hers.

"I do love you," he said again.

A knock sounded on the door. Not a polite tap but an impatient summons.

Marissa's gaze moved from the door to the phone, which had started to ring again. The cell in his pocket was also vibrating, though she couldn't know that.

"So far none of this is what I feared," she said. "So why don't you tell me what I'm missing?"

Before he could respond, the door opened.

"Dante—" Matt visibly winced when he saw that Marissa was in the room. "I'm sorry to interrupt," he said to the princess. "But I need to speak with my brother. It's extremely important."

But Dante didn't need Matteo to tell him what he already knew.

The urgency of the ringing phones and his brother's appearance at his door within days of receiving that package from Naomi could only mean that she'd followed through on her threat. And that somehow, in the short span of time between when Dante met Marissa at the airport and now, the photos had gone viral.

Chapter Fourteen

Marissa didn't think she'd ever seen Dante sweat. But she could see it now, the light sheen of perspiration on his brow, the tension in his tightly clenched jaw, the pleading in his eyes. And the warmth that had flooded her system when he'd told her he loved her suddenly turned to ice.

"What's going on, Dante?"

The phone in her purse was ringing now, too, but she didn't reach for it. She somehow knew that her call was connected to the ringing of his phone and his brother's presence, but she didn't want to hear the answer from anyone but Dante.

She glanced at the prince, who was still hovering in the doorway and looking at her with pity and apology in his eyes.

"Photos?" It was the only word Dante spoke to Matt.

His brother nodded.

"I need some time with my fiancée," the king said.

"Of course," Matt agreed and backed out, closing the door behind him.

The phone on the desk had stopped ringing again, but her cell continued to chime. She pulled it out of her purse and turned it off. The sudden silence in the room was ominous.

"Photos?" she asked, her voice little more than a whisper.

He swallowed. "It was before I met you."

"What was before you met me?"

"It was a fling. A one-night stand."

Her eyes filled with tears.

"I'm sorry," he said. "I didn't want you to find out this way."

"If it was before you met me, why does it matter?" she asked, even though she knew that it did. Dante's past exploits were hardly a secret, but she was his fiancée now—

She looked down at the ring on her finger.

I chose to give you that ring...because I fell in love with you.

"It doesn't," he said, as if he could make her believe it. "Not to me. But there will be talk, speculation that I was with her when I was engaged to you, that I cheated on you."

"Who is she?"

He ran his hands through his hair. "I don't know."

"How can you not..." The question trailed off as a sudden, startling thought came to her.

Was it possible that he was talking about the night of the Mythos Ball? The night she was almost certain that they had spent together?

"Who took the photos?"

"I don't know," he said again. "I'd guess Naomi or someone she knows, because copies were delivered to me a few days ago."

"I want to see them."

He winced. "Marissa—"

"Aren't they all over the internet by now, anyway?"

"Probably," he admitted reluctantly.

She waited while he went over to his desk, unlocked the bottom drawer and pulled out a large envelope.

Her fingers were trembling as she took the package from him. If she was right, the pictures inside would be of Juno and Jupiter. If she was wrong...

Her stomach churned at the thought. If she was wrong, she would find herself looking at pictures of Dante and another woman, maybe touching that other woman, kissing her and even making love with her.

She'd rather know than speculate.

She opened the flap and tipped out the photos.

And her heart started beating again.

Dante didn't want to see the shock and hurt and betrayal on her face when she looked at the pictures, but he couldn't seem to look away.

He heard the sharp intake of her breath as the photos spilled out of the envelope. Yep, there was the shock. She sifted through the images, scrutinizing each one closely enough that her study made him uneasy.

He waited for her to rage, to cry, to throw something at him. But after she'd looked at all of the photos, she put them back in the envelope and said, "I know who she is."

"Whoever she is, you have to believe that I didn't go to the ball looking to hook up with someone," he said, desperate for her to trust him. "In fact, I only went because I thought you would be there."

"Instead you met Juno."

He should have realized that she would recognize the peacock feathers in the mask as one of the goddess's trademarks because of her association with the Juno's Touch project at PACH.

"The mythos theme for the ball was my idea," she told him now. "The costumes were my idea. And I was Juno."

He stared at her, stunned. He wanted to believe what she said was true, but it seemed too incredible.

"She had red hair and green eyes—" he shook his head, startled by what was so patently obvious to him now "—easy enough to fake with a wig and colored contacts."

She nodded.

"You knew," he said, startled anew by this realization. "You knew that I was Jupiter, that I was the man you made love with that night, and you didn't tell me?"

"I only figured it out a few days ago," she told him, clearly on the defensive now. "Before I left for Tesoro del Mar, when I went into your office to write a note, I knocked your agenda off of the desk and found a peacock feather in it."

He didn't know how he was supposed to respond or even how he was supposed to feel. Was it appropriate to feel relief that he hadn't been with someone else? To feel shock that the woman he had been with was the woman he loved? But he had to set aside the shock, and he knew that any sense of relief was premature because discovering the real identity of Juno wasn't going to make the scandal of the photos go away.

"What are we going to do now?" Marissa asked, apparently having tracked the direction of his thoughts. "How are we supposed to respond to something like this?"

"I'm sure my advisers are already meeting with the palace's media liaison to figure out all the potential angles," he told her. "Right now, I see a couple of possibilities. We can ignore the photos and trust that something bigger and juicier will take over the headlines by the end of the week. Or I can make an official statement acknowledging that those are photos of me taken the night of the masquerade ball and asserting that there has been no one else in my life since I met you."

"Or we could call a press conference where I show up in

Juno's costume to put an end to the speculation once and for all."

"No way." His response was as definite as it was immediate.

"Why not?"

"Because I know how much you hate being the center of any kind of media attention and this will be the worst possible kind." In fact, knowing how strongly she felt about avoiding publicity, he was shocked that she would ever come up with such a plan.

"I wouldn't have chosen to go public with the information," she admitted. "But you can't honestly expect me to remain in the shadows now that those photos are everywhere."

"Those photos were taken because Naomi was targeting *me*. There's no reason to drag you into the middle of this."

"No reason except that I'm already in the middle of it."

He shook his head. "I can't completely isolate you from the fallout, but I can—and will—ensure you're protected as much as possible. And there is absolutely no way I'm involving you in a sex scandal."

"They're sexy pictures," she said. "But not *sex* pictures."

"The distinction isn't going to mean much to the reporters shouting questions at you and photographers blinding you with flashbulbs."

"I don't need you to protect me, Dante. I need you to let me stand by your side, to show the world that we are united."

"But why would you want to? I know this whole scenario is a nightmare for you."

"Because I love you," she said simply.

The words rocked him to the core. Stunned him. Humbled him.

He touched his forehead to hers. "I don't deserve you," he said. "But I am so incredibly grateful for you."

She wrapped her arms around his waist, holding him tight. "And I will stand by your side, for now and forever," she vowed. "But I won't be tucked away and then taken out when it suits your purposes. I need to be your partner. I need you to know that I will always be there for you."

"I want you by my side," he said. "But you can't blame me for wanting to protect you."

"I don't blame you," she assured him. "I'm just telling you that I won't accept it."

"I guess that means we're going to do a press conference—together."

Less than twenty-four hours after Matteo knocked on the door of Dante's suite, Dante and Marissa stood together outside the front gates of the palace to issue their joint statement to the media.

Marissa knew the ripple effects would continue for a while, but they'd done what they could and from this point on, they just had to ride out the waves. Dante took her hand, guiding her away from the crowd. The festively decorated gates closed behind them, shutting out the reporters and photographers. But cameras continued to flash, capturing every step as they made their way, hand in hand, back to the palace.

"Well, that's done," Dante said, careful to keep his voice low.

Marissa could only breathe a slow and shaky sigh of relief. She didn't want him to know how absolutely terrified she'd been, or that she was still shaking on the inside. But she'd faced down the reporters without batting an eyelash—and without throwing up. She figured if she could face that rabid pack of reporters with such a meaty story, anything else she would encounter would be a piece of cake.

Of course, Dante had done all the talking, reading a joint statement that had been carefully prepared and meticulously proofed. They were advised not to take any questions, since they weren't prepared to lie about the events of that night and the king's advisers didn't want either of them to admit they hadn't even exchanged names before they'd gotten naked together.

Dante squeezed her hand. "You survived your first trial by fire," he said reassuringly.

"Hopefully my first and last," she said.

Waiting at the top of the steps behind the balustrade draped with an evergreen garland, were all of Dante's family. Benedicto stood tall, clasping Arianna's hand in his own. They were flanked by their other four children, with Jovanni and Leticia on one side and Francesca and Matteo on the other. The decorated evergreen trees lined up in the background made it appear as if they were posing for a Christmas greeting card, reminding Marissa that—despite everything else that had happened over the past few days—the holidays were rapidly approaching.

But it wasn't the decor that had snagged her attention— it was the Romero family's unexpected show of support. Marissa hadn't realized they were there—truthfully, she wished they hadn't had to witness any of what had been revealed in the past twenty-four hours. Seeing them now, her eyes filled with tears.

Her own family was, by virtue of being in Tesoro del Mar, more removed from the situation. But for the citizens of Ardena, there was no distance or objectivity. Dante was their king—the head of their government, ambassador of their nation and supposed role model for future generations. And the effects of his behavior were real and immediate.

Marissa feared that for Benedicto and Arianna and their children the situation was even more personal. To them, Dante wasn't just the king of Ardena; he was their son and their brother. Despite the public show of support, she couldn't help but fear that they were privately disappointed.

It was Arianna who broke the silence when they reached the top of the steps, but only to say, "Come, Marissa. The dressmaker is here for final approval on your wedding gown design."

It was exactly the distraction she needed to push the press conference out of her mind, if only for a little while. She reviewed the sketches, suggested a few minor changes. Her measurements were double-checked, the designer clucking her disapproval about brides unnecessarily dropping pounds and dresses requiring last-minute adjustments.

"I'm sorry," Marissa said to Arianna when the designer had gone.

Dante's mother looked genuinely puzzled. "Whatever are you apologizing for?"

"For my selfish and reckless behavior."

Arianna perched on the edge of the stool in front of Marissa and took both of her hands. "You are one of the most selfless and considerate people I've ever known," she said sincerely. "But no one goes through life without making mistakes. Fortunately, most people don't have to worry that those mistakes will be broadcast to the world and judged by those who have no right to judge. Unfortunately for you, as a princess and soon-to-be queen, you don't fall into the category of 'most people.'"

"I thought you'd be angry."

"I'm furious," the queen promised. "But not with you, and not even with Dante, although this admittedly isn't his first… indiscretion."

Marissa managed a smile at that.

"And I'm grateful that you were there with my son today."

"Where else would I have been?"

"I imagine, if Dante had been given a choice, you would

have been safely tucked inside the palace, away from the cameras and questions."

"Obviously you know your son well."

"He is a lot like his father, sometimes frustratingly so." Arianna released her hands abruptly and stood up. "Your designer was asking about the jewelry you planned to wear with your dress."

"I haven't given it much thought."

The queen moved to the dresser and picked up a burgundy velvet box. "Well, perhaps you'd like to think about these."

She opened the lid, revealing a pair of stunning chandelier-style diamond earrings.

"My mother-in-law gave them to me on my wedding day," Arianna told her. "For me, they were 'something new.' If you'd like to wear them, they could be your 'something borrowed.'"

Marissa's eyes blurred. "I would very much like to wear them. Thank you."

When Marissa left the queen's rooms, she was advised by one of Dante's assistants that the king wished to see her in his private office. She hadn't planned to seek him out, assuming that he'd be in strategy meetings for the rest of the day, but she was glad he'd asked for her. As difficult as it had been for Marissa to face the hoard of reporters, she knew it had been even harder for the king, who felt he had disappointed his people, and she wanted to make sure he was okay.

She knocked on the door.

"Come in."

He was at his desk, but he didn't seem to be focused on the papers spread out in front of him. When she stepped through the door, his gaze zeroed in on her and the weight on his shoulders seemed to lift a little.

"I didn't think it would take that long to measure you for one wedding dress," he said, rising from his chair.

"I spent a few minutes with your mother when the fitting was done."

"Are you okay?"

"Don't I look relatively unscathed?"

His smile was wry as he reached for her hands. "I didn't mean after your chat with my mother but after the press conference."

"I'm okay." She tipped her head back to meet his gaze. "How about you?"

"I'm much better now," he said and touched his lips gently to hers.

"Is that why I'm here—because you felt the need to check up on me?"

"No, you're here because, after bleeding out the most personal details of my life to the public, I wanted some time alone with you," he told her.

"To talk?" she asked lightly.

He smiled as he turned the handle of the door that separated his office from his bedroom. "I know there are still things to be said, and I want you to know that I'm sorry for all of this and grateful that you were there with me today, but no. Right now, I don't want to talk. I just want to hold you."

She turned willingly into his embrace.

Dante held on tight, breathing in her scent, relishing the warm softness of her body pressed against him.

But eventually the need to both take and offer comfort turned into something stronger, deeper and more demanding. Desire stirred in his belly, pulsed in his veins. With Marissa's body tucked so closely against his, she couldn't fail to notice that he was aroused. Which she proved when she asked, "Are you sure you just want to hold me?"

He chuckled softly. "Maybe I want more than that."

"I want you to make love with me, Dante." She tipped her head back to look at him, those beautiful gold eyes swirling with emotion. "I want to be with you more than anything else in the world. And after everything that's happened in the past twenty-four hours, I think we should cherish every minute we have together."

He cupped her face gently in his palms, stroked his thumbs gently over her cheeks. "I'm not going to argue with that."

"But I'm scared," she admitted. "The first night we made love, I was scared because I didn't know what to expect. The next day, I was scared because I was certain that I would never see you again, and I knew that no one else could ever make me feel the way I felt when I was in your arms. Now I'm scared because what I feel for you is so much more than I ever expected."

"We're on equal ground there," he promised her. "I've been with other women, but I've never felt about anyone else the way I feel about you."

"I've only ever been with you," she reminded him softly.

With everything else that had been going on, his brain had somehow failed to make that connection.

"I was your first lover," he said and felt a surge of what could only be described as primal satisfaction. She was his, had always been his and would always be his.

"My only lover."

He touched his lips to hers. "The only one you're ever going to know."

"The only one I want," she promised him.

"For the past several weeks, I've been thinking about our first time together, wanting to make sure it was perfect for you, without realizing we've already had our first time together."

"And it was perfect," she assured him.

"I can do better."

She smiled at the eagerness of his claim. "Do you think so?"

"I know so."

"Then take me to bed, Dante, and show me."

"Is that a personal request or a royal command?"

She smiled again and he knew she was remembering the day she'd asked that same question of him—albeit in a different context—and his response.

"Whatever gets you naked with me," she told him.

He scooped her into his arms.

Chapter Fifteen

Dante lowered Marissa gently onto the mattress, then he slowly and methodically began to remove her clothes.

He started with the plum-colored jacket. He held her gaze as he undid the first and then the second gold button, then tossed it aside. There were a lot more buttons down the front of her ivory-colored blouse. Tiny pearl buttons that he slipped out of the little loops of satin that held them secure, one by one. He spread the two sides apart to reveal a bronze-colored lace fantasy that barely covered the soft swell of her breasts. With a groan of pure male appreciation, he lowered his head to press his lips to her collarbone, to the hollow between her breasts, to the pale, tender skin just above her belly button.

He reached beneath her for the zipper at the back of her skirt, slowly slid it downward, then tugged the skirt over her hips, down the length of her legs. He'd expected that her underwear would match the bra—he hadn't expected a coordinating garter belt, too. He tossed the skirt aside with her jacket, his attention riveted by the contrast of bronze lace and ivory skin and barely there silk stockings. His fingertips traced the scalloped band at the top of her stockings, carefully following the contours, and she quivered. He reached around to the back of her thighs to release the clips there, then returned to the front and undid those, as well. Then he rolled her stockings, one by one, down her legs and discarded them with the suit.

"You are..." For a moment, words actually failed him. And though he didn't think the description did her justice, he finally settled on "spectacular."

She smiled, pleased by his compliment, but he could see the lingering hint of nerves in her eyes.

He discarded his jacket, pants, shirt and socks, but decided it wasn't just smart but necessary to keep his briefs on for the moment. She watched as he stripped away his clothes, her gaze roaming avidly over his body. When he joined her on the bed again, she reached for him, her hands stroking over his chest, his shoulders, his back.

"I've dreamed of touching you like this," she told him. "Of feeling the warmth of your skin beneath my palms. Of your body pressed against mine. Moving inside me."

Her words lit a fire in his veins. He captured her mouth, kissing her deeply, hungrily. She moaned in pleasure and arched against him so that her breasts brushed against his chest, her pelvis against his groin. He gritted his teeth, trying to control his body's instinctive reaction to her sensual movements. Two more minutes of her body rubbing against his and he would go off like a novice inside his briefs.

He captured those eager hands, cuffing her wrists and holding them over her head. She pouted, just a little, and he couldn't resist nipping at the sexy fullness of her bottom lip. She moaned softly, her eyes closing as her back arched, pressing her torso more fully against his.

"You are dangerous, woman."

Her lips curved now, the slow, sexy smile of a woman who knew she was in control.

He was determined to change that.

He shifted so that his knees were straddling her thighs, then lowered his head to her breast. He rubbed his lips over the peak of her nipple straining against the lace, and her breath hitched. He let his teeth scrape along the same path and felt the air shudder out of her lungs. Then her took the turgid peak in his mouth and suckled her through the delicate fabric, and her whole body shuddered.

He shifted his attention to the other breast and repeated the pattern until she was breathless and trembling. Then he released the clasp at her back and slowly drew the straps down her arms, uncovering just a hint of her pale skin, then a little bit more and a little bit more again, until her breasts were completely bared to his hungry gaze.

And then he used his lips and his tongue and his teeth again, to sample and savor the flavor of her naked flesh. While his mouth was busy with her breasts, his hands skimmed down her torso, following her curves and contours. Her quick, shallow breaths warned that she was close to the edge as he stripped away the garter, then slid a hand down the front of her bikinis. She gasped at the intimacy of the contact as his fingers sifted through the soft curls and flew apart when he found her center.

He shifted away from her only long enough to yank off his briefs and tug her bikinis down over her hips. He didn't wait for the aftershocks to fade, but eased into her while her body was still shuddering. Her second orgasm followed immediately on the heels of the first, her inner muscles clamping around him like a vice, and the rhythmic pulsing nearly pulled him over the edge with her.

He fisted his hands in the sheet, waiting for the waves of

her release to subside, as he was swamped by emotions far deeper than any he'd ever imagined.

He'd already told her he loved her, because he knew that he did. But when he sank into her, when she opened up and took him inside, he felt a soul-deep connection he'd never known before.

Because no one had ever bothered to look into his heart as Marissa had done. She'd taken the time to know him and understand him, and despite all of his flaws and faults, she'd accepted him and loved him. And because she did, the experience of making love with her was all the more intimate.

It wasn't just the physical joining of two bodies, but the mating of two hearts, the merging of two souls.

It was a long time after before Marissa could move, not that she wanted to go anywhere. She was more than happy to be right where she was, tucked close to Dante's body. Her head was on his shoulder and her hand was over his heart, absorbing the rhythm of each steady beat.

"You were right," she said when she finally summoned the energy to speak.

He touched his lips to her forehead. "About?"

"That was better."

"Told you."

She heard the smugness in his tone and suspected he was wearing the familiar cocky grin she'd come to know so well, but she was too lazy to tip her head back to confirm her suspicion.

"Do me a favor?" she asked.

"What's that?"

"Remind me never to challenge you to prove something again—I don't think I could survive it."

"I bet you could."

Her breath caught in her throat when his hand closed over her breast.

She'd honestly thought she was sated. Not just satisfied but completely spent. But all it had taken was one touch and desire coursed through her system anew.

"Dante." She wasn't sure if it was a plea or a warning.

His only response was to shift so that she was once again beneath him. Then he rubbed his lips against hers, nibbling, teasing.

"I bet you could," he repeated.

And, once again, he was right.

The headlines weren't quite what she expected.

Not just unexpected but disappointing. The people of Ardena should have been clamoring for the Casanova king to step down; instead, they were suddenly fascinated by the "obvious passion" between their ruler and his soon-to-be bride, turning the tawdry events of that night into a chapter in some great love story.

Tears burned the back of her eyes.

It wasn't fair. He was supposed to pay for what he'd done to Fiona, for abandoning her and walking away from his own child.

Her phone beeped. She opened the message:
r u there? on my way home, big news 2 share
She texted back: im here
And waited to see what news her sister had now.

Almost a month after the photos were first posted online, interest in the sexy pictures of the king and his fiancée had faded but not completely died. But there had been other scandals around the world and more important issues to deal with at home.

Dante's timely intervention had helped negotiate an agreement between the Minister of the Environment and the Fisheries Union that kept the fishermen on the water and had them singing their praises of the king. Dr. Kalidindi had been vocal in his appreciation of the princess's help with the new volunteer-cuddler program at Mercy Medical Center, and the general consensus was that the king had made a good choice in his soon-to-be queen.

Overall, Marissa felt confident that the storm had been weathered. And now the country was gearing up for the royal wedding, just two weeks away, and the Christmas holiday after that. As she waited for Dante, admiring the effect of the twinkling lights wrapped around the hedges that bordered the courtyard, the absolute last person on her mind was Naomi Breslin. She certainly didn't think there was any possibility the girl would have the nerve to seek her out. Nor did she think there was any way Naomi would ever get past the front gates of the property. So she was both shocked and distressed to see her in the courtyard.

"I sometimes worked as a server when extra help was needed for big events," Naomi explained before Marissa could even ask, then voluntarily handed over her security pass.

Marissa tucked it in her pocket. "What are you doing here?"

"I wanted to apologize."

"An apology can't undo what you did," she told her.

"I know, but—" The rest of the words seemed to get stuck in her throat when she saw Dante coming toward them.

"I've called security," he told Naomi. "You're lucky I didn't call the police."

She just nodded, her eyes filling with tears. "I needed to see you, to tell you how sorry I am." Then she reached into the pocket of her jeans and pulled out a folded piece of paper. "And I wanted you to see this."

"If this is another photo—" Dante warned, taking the page from her.

Her cheeks flushed. "No. It's a copy of Siobhan's paternity test."

He handed it back without even looking at it.

"You don't want to know who her father is?"

"It has nothing to do with me, because there was never any possibility that she was mine."

"I know that now," Naomi admitted. "My sister told me everything when Rico came back."

Marissa assumed Rico must be the baby's father, and while the revelation of this information couldn't change anything, it did give her hope that she and Dante might be able to move forward with their lives without always worrying that Naomi might be lurking around the next corner, trying to cause trouble for them.

"I tried to ruin your life because I thought you'd ruined hers." She glanced down at Dante's and Marissa's joined hands. "I'm glad I didn't succeed."

Then she curtsied to the king and his fiancée and turned to meet the guards who had arrived to escort her off of the property.

"Well, that was…surprising," Marissa said.

"And surprisingly insightful," Dante said.

"You could have her arrested."

"I could," he agreed. "But it wouldn't accomplish anything. Besides, she was right."

"About the fact that she tried to ruin your life?"

He shook his head. "About the fact that she didn't succeed. She wanted to create a scandal so huge, I would lose the throne. But when I saw those pictures, the only possibility that scared me was the possibility of losing you."

Marissa kissed him lightly. "That's never going to happen."

"And that's why she didn't succeed. Because as long as I have you, I have everything that matters."

For Marissa, the final days leading up to the wedding were a frantic carousel of fittings and Christmas shopping and packing for the honeymoon and double-checking all the details for the big day. The nights in Dante's arm were her respite—a chance for her to finally pause long enough to catch her breath and revel in the exquisite lovemaking of the man who would soon be her husband.

But she spent the night of December twentieth alone in her own room, to uphold the tradition that the groom should not see his bride before the wedding. But she wasn't completely alone. Dante's sisters rounded up the girls—their mother, Marissa's mother, Gabby and Hannah—who had come to Ardena with their families for the occasion and were also staying at the palace—and stopped by with a couple of bottles of champagne.

Actually, they had two bottles of champagne and a bottle of sparkling grape juice, the nonalcoholic version intended for Hannah, who was in her fifth month of pregnancy, and Gabby, who was nursing seven-week-old Talisa. The children were also in attendance, of course, but Sierra was keeping an eye on the little ones in the guest wing.

Francesca claimed the wine was part of a traditional celebration of a bride-to-be's last night as a single woman. Leticia said she didn't care about the tradition—any night was a good night for bubbly. Marissa discreetly tipped her champagne into the pot of the poinsettia tree in her sitting room and refilled her glass from the other bottle. Though she didn't yet know for sure, she thought it was possible that the recent tenderness in her breasts and increased fatigue might be early signs of pregnancy and she didn't want to take any chances if she was lucky enough to already have a new life growing inside of her.

But even if she wasn't yet pregnant, Marissa couldn't help but feel as if she was the luckiest woman in the world. It was the night before her wedding to the man she loved with all of her heart, and she was fortunate enough to spend it with four friends who would all be her sisters by virtue of marriage, the soon-to-be mother-in-law who had graciously welcomed her into the family and her own mother. And if Elena's presence wasn't the highlight of her night, at least her mother did nothing to spoil the occasion.

While Marissa faked drinking champagne with the girls, Dante was sipping brandy with the men—his father, his brothers and Marissa's brothers. He'd had some apprehension about meeting Michael and Cameron—after all, he was indirectly responsible for scandalous pictures of their little sister being posted on the internet—but they'd reassured him that they wouldn't put any visible bruises on him before the wedding since he was doing the honorable thing by marrying Marissa. Dante thought he scored some points, and saved himself some grief, by telling them that he wasn't marrying Marissa because it was the right thing to do, but because he loved her with his whole heart.

Before the brandy decanter was empty, Cameron excused himself for the night, eager to get back to his own room and check on his children. Michael followed his brother.

"I remember what it was like to be a new father," Benedicto mused. "The excitement, the nervousness and the indescribable joy of having a child who is the best parts of both parents."

"He's talking about when I was born," Matt teased his brothers. "Because I'm the only one who is a combination of all the best parts."

Van, because he was closest, cuffed the side of his brother's head. Dante just chuckled.

"You all inherited different characteristics and traits," Benedicto said. "But when each of you is lucky enough to hold your own child in your arms, and hopefully that won't be too far in the future—" he sent a pointed luck in Dante's direction "—you'll appreciate how a parent's love for a child never falters, even when that child is exhibiting some of the not-so-good parts."

Dante didn't say anything to encourage his father's hopes, but he suspected that his parents weren't going to have to wait much more than nine months for the grandchild they both coveted, if even that.

And with those last words, the old king hugged his son and wished him a good-night. Van walked out with his father, leaving only Matt with the groom-to-be.

"Last chance to make a break for it," his little brother said, only half teasing. "If you go now, you've got quite a few hours before anyone would even notice you were gone."

Dante just shook his head, because he knew that a life with Marissa was his best chance for the happily-ever-after he never thought he would have.

The morning of December twenty-first dawned clear and bright and unseasonably cold.

But Marissa didn't worry about the weather. She didn't care about anything except that today was the day she was going to become Dante's wife. Of course, their marriage would also elevate her status from that of princess to queen, but she decided she had enough butterflies in her stomach without thinking about that. Or maybe the slight queasiness was something more than butterflies.

She was afraid to hope. Afraid to want anything more when she was already so incredibly blessed.

But a baby...Dante's baby. It was impossible to even think those words without a smile spreading across her face.

She was still smiling when Gabriella snuck into her room and tucked a flat, narrow box into the pocket of her robe. Marissa didn't ask why and her sister-in-law didn't say. She just kissed the bride's cheek and slipped out again.

Marissa was grateful they'd opted for an early-afternoon ceremony, so that she didn't have any time to sit around and wait. In fact, she barely had time to nibble on a piece of toast and sip a cup of tea before she was surrounded by people fussing over her hair and touching up her makeup.

When she was finally groomed and polished and dressed, her mother came into her room. Her gaze moved from the pile of curls on top of Marissa's head to the peep-toe sandals on her feet, and Marissa instinctively braced herself. But she was completely unprepared when Elena, her eyes shimmering with moisture, said, "You truly are the most beautiful bride I've ever seen."

It was the sincerity in her tone even more than the unexpected compliment that made Marissa's throat tight. She managed a shaky smile. "And you're the most beautiful mother of the bride."

Elena picked up Marissa's bouquet of white calla lilies tied with a wide satin ribbon and handed it to her daughter. "I do want you to be happy."

Of course, the words sounded more like a royal command than a wish, but Marissa appreciated them nonetheless.

"I already am," she said and meant it.

Her mother gave her a quick hug, the impulsive gesture of affection even more unexpected than the kind words.

"In that case, we better get to the church. We don't want to keep your groom waiting."

The church was decorated in royal fashion for the holiday wedding of Ardena's king and the Tesorian princess. In addition to the enormous wreath over the arched entranceway, there were evergreen garlands wrapped around the balcony railings. Gold bows marked the ends of the pews and a mountain of Christmas flowers bordered the steps to the alter. But Dante had barely noticed any of the decorations. He was waiting for his bride, and not very patiently.

Now that the day was finally here, he wanted it to be done. He wanted Marissa as his wife so they could officially start their life together.

Then, finally, she was there. The first glimpse of his bride at the back of the church simply took his breath away.

He didn't know enough about bridal fashions to recognize that the Roman-inspired asymmetrical dress was made of layers of snowy chiffon with a wide band of beading at the empire-style waist. He just knew that she was absolutely stunning. And with every step she took toward him, the joy in his heart continued to swell until it overflowed and filled every part of him.

She was his bride. His goddess. His heart.

And when he spoke his vows, he didn't hesitate or falter. Although the words had been spoken by countless grooms before him, he felt as if they'd been written from his heart. And when it was Marissa's turn, her gaze was just as steady, her voice as clear.

Church bells were ringing in celebration of the union of Ardena's king and his new queen as they exited the church... just in time to see the first flakes of snow begin to fall from the sky.

"You told me it wouldn't snow," the bride said.

"What I said was that the forecasters were probably wrong when they predicted snow because it hasn't snowed in this part of the country in more than fifteen years," her groom reminded her.

"It's snowing now."

"Which proves that today is a day of miracles."

"More than you probably know," she murmured, a smile playing at the corners of her mouth.

His gaze dipped to her belly as anticipation jumped in his own. "Baby?" He barely mouthed the word, wanting to ensure his question couldn't possibly be overheard.

She nodded, her eyes filled with both joy and uncertainty.

He knew how eager she was to start a family, so he guessed that any hesitation she was experiencing was a result of not knowing how he would respond to the news. He was more than happy to reassure her. "That is absolutely the best Christmas present you could give me."

Her lips curved. "In that case, Merry Christmas, Your Majesty."

And then, right there at the top of the steps and with thousands of jubilant Ardenans watching, the king kissed his queen.

Epilogue

KING DANTE WEDS TESORIAN PRINCESS
by Alex Girard

Snow is an extremely rare occurrence in Saint Georgios. Such a rare occurrence, in fact, that any amount of snowfall would usually be front-page news. But on the first official day of winter, not even a blizzard could have upstaged the pre-Christmas nuptials of His Majesty the King Dante Romero of Ardena to Her Highness Princess Marissa Leandres of Tesoro del Mar.

Just as the bells of Sacred Heart began to toll in celebration of their marriage, the people who had braved the unseasonably cold weather to line the streets in the hopes of catching a glimpse of the king and his new queen were treated to a lovely display of fluffy white flakes swirling in the sky—and then, the lovelier image of the bride as she exited the church with her groom.

It was a picture-perfect moment, made even more perfect when the royal couple shared their first kiss as husband and wife and the crowd roared its approval.

The royal wedding was a celebration for the whole nation, but it was also very much a family affair. The bride was attended by both of the groom's sisters, Princesses Francesca and Leticia, and her niece Princess Sierra, with another niece, Princess Riley, as her flower girl. The groom's best man was his father, and his brothers, Princes Jovanni and Matteo, performed ushering duties.

In the midst of all of the carefully orchestrated pageantry, there were moments of spontaneity (the flower girl climbing the cake table to see the decorations at the very top), and possibly some hints of romance on the horizon (the groom's youngest brother danced mostly with the bride's eldest niece). And by the time the cake was cut and the dancing was done, the snow had stopped falling.

But it was evident to anyone who witnessed the exchange of vows that the newlyweds weren't worried about the weather...they were just looking forward to their holiday honeymoon.

* * * * *

HEART & HOME

Heartwarming romances where love can
happen right when you least expect it.

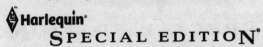

SPECIAL EDITION

COMING NEXT MONTH
AVAILABLE DECEMBER 27, 2011

#2161 FORTUNE'S CINDERELLA
The Fortunes of Texas: Whirlwind Romance
Karen Templeton

#2162 MOMMY IN THE MAKING
Northbridge Nuptials
Victoria Pade

#2163 DOCTORS IN THE WEDDING
Doctors in the Family
Gina Wilkins

#2164 THE DADDY DANCE
Mindy Klasky

#2165 THE HUSBAND RECIPE
Linda Winstead Jones

#2166 MADE FOR MARRIAGE
Helen Lacey

SPECIAL EDITION

Life, Love and Family

Karen Templeton

introduces

The FORTUNES *of* TEXAS: Whirlwind Romance

When a tornado destroys Red Rock, Texas, Christina Hastings finds herself trapped in the rubble with telecommunications heir Scott Fortune. He's handsome, smart and everything Christina has learned to guard herself against. As they await rescue, an unlikely attraction forms between the two and Scott soon finds himself wanting to know about this mysterious beauty. But can he catch Christina before she runs away from her true feelings?

FORTUNE'S CINDERELLA

Available December 27th wherever books are sold!

*Brittany Grayson survived a horrible ordeal at the hands
of a serial killer known as The Professional…
who's after her now?*

*Harlequin® Romantic Suspense presents a new installment
in Carla Cassidy's reader-favorite miniseries,*
LAWMEN OF BLACK ROCK.

Enjoy a sneak peek of
TOOL BELT DEFENDER.

*Available January 2012
from Harlequin® Romantic Suspense.*

"**B**rittany?" His voice was deep and pleasant and made
her realize she'd been staring at him openmouthed through
the screen door.

"Yes, I'm Brittany and you must be…" Her mind suddenly went blank.

"Alex. Alex Crawford, Chad's friend. You called him
about a deck?"

As she unlocked the screen, she realized she wasn't
quite ready yet to allow a stranger inside, especially a male
stranger.

"Yes, I did. It's nice to meet you, Alex. Let's walk around
back and I'll show you what I have in mind," she said. She
frowned as she realized there was no car in her driveway.
"Did you walk here?" she asked.

His eyes were a warm blue that stood out against his
tanned face and was complemented by his slightly shaggy
dark hair. "I live three doors up." He pointed up the street to
the Walker home that had been on the market for a while.

"How long have you lived there?"

"I moved in about six weeks ago," he replied as they

walked around the side of the house.

That explained why she didn't know the Walkers had moved out and Mr. Hard Body had moved in. Six weeks ago she'd still been living at her brother Benjamin's house trying to heal from the trauma she'd lived through.

As they reached the backyard she motioned toward the broken brick patio just outside the back door. "What I'd like is a wooden deck big enough to hold a barbecue pit and an umbrella table and, of course, lots of people."

He nodded and pulled a tape measure from his tool belt. "An outdoor entertainment area," he said.

"Exactly," she replied and watched as he began to walk the site. The last thing Brittany had wanted to think about over the past eight months of her life was men. But looking at Alex Crawford definitely gave her a slight flutter of pure feminine pleasure.

Will Brittany be able to heal in the arms of Alex, her hotter-than-sin handyman…or will a second psychopath silence her forever? Find out in
TOOL BELT DEFENDER
Available January 2012
from Harlequin® Romantic Suspense
wherever books are sold.

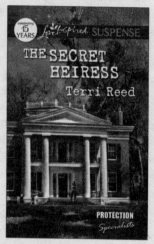